JIMMY LAVENDER, CHICAGO DETECTIVE

Jimmy Lavender — Chicago Detective. The name conjures images of gangland murders, Al Capone and illegal bootleg whiskey, but Lavender has more in common with Sherlock Holmes. In some of his most baffling cases, Lavender comes up against such brain-twisters as a marble fountain statue that seemingly comes to life and walks by night; a fiancé who goes missing on the eve of his wedding; a missing sack of uncut diamonds; and murder, robbery, and sudden death on the high seas!

VINCENT STARRETT

Edited by John Betancourt

<hr />

JIMMY LAVENDER, CHICAGO DETECTIVE

Complete and Unabridged

LINFORD
Leicester

First published in Great Britain

First Linford Edition
published 2014

A catalogue record for this book is available
from the British Library.

ISBN 978–1–4448–1834–5

Published by
F. A. Thorpe (Publishing)
Anstey, Leicestershire

Set by Words & Graphics Ltd.
Anstey, Leicestershire
Printed and bound in Great Britain by
T. J. International Ltd., Padstow, Cornwall

This book is printed on acid-free paper

The Fugitive Statue

1

Mr. Oakley Ashenhurst removed his pipe from his mouth with his left hand, and with a lift of his chin blew a cloud of smoke at the ceiling of his study. His right hand held open the volume he had been reading spread out upon the table; in the circle of bright light dropped upon the pages by the young man's student lamp, the black print seemed doubly black.

Ashenhurst yawned luxuriously and lay back in his chair. The corners of his study, which was also his bedroom, sitting room, library, and — on furtive occasions — his dining room, were deeply dark with a darkness that lightened by degrees as it approached the spot occupied by the reading table and the funnel of intense light from the lamp. Upon a low mantel ticked a nickel-plated clock, and by a swift movement of the ingenious lamp the student ascertained that it was exactly midnight. At this instant, while he was registering satisfaction and relief, in the street beyond his window Oakley Ashenhurst heard the sound of running feet.

They were steady footsteps, light but sharp, and they slapped the pavement with a staccato quality that was impressive in the silence. They approached, crescendoed before the house, and diminuendoed in the distance, as drumsticks simulate hoof beats in the theatre. Reclined in his chair, young Ashenhurst heard them come and heard them go with idle curiosity. Hazy speculations floated through his mind for a few moments; then with an effort he pulled himself together, marked his place in the volume, snapped off the light, and slipped out of his bathrobe and into his bed. In the morning, he thought nothing about the footsteps at all; he had forgotten them.

But the next night, after a harrowing session at the evening medical class in which he was completing his education, as he toiled again over his *Anatomy* in the darkened room, the young man's memory was jogged; he was reminded by the footsteps themselves. As before, they approached with soft distinctness, pattered sharply past the dark dwelling, and melted away in the silence.

Ashenhurst's mind stirred sleepily. Last night — midnight — very curious!

He turned the light funnel on the little clock and registered mild surprise. Again it was midnight! An odd coincidence, thought Ashenhurst as he climbed into bed. Somebody in training for a race? The nights were getting cool for track suits, he thought with a chuckle. And anyway, why this short, deserted thoroughfare with its straggle of sickly street lamps and its old-fashioned, sober dwellings? Why not the fine stretches of the neighboring boulevard? Or, for that matter, the little park at the corner, with its cinder paths seemingly designed for such an enterprise? He was still speculating when he fell asleep.

As he crossed the park the next morning on his way to the office, young Mr. Ashenhurst thought again of the footsteps. Decidedly these cinder paths were the proper lanes for training. As a young man on the very brink of becoming a physician, Ashenhurst approved the activities of the midnight sprinter, but as a methodical young man he believed that a sense of fitness should direct the activity; and decidedly these cinder paths were preferable to hard asphalt. He paused for a moment beside the central fountain to admire the graceful figure of the faun from whose upturned pipes, the water burst like iridescent flute notes; he dabbled his fingers in the pool and tossed crumbs to the stately couple — Mr. and Mrs. Swan he always called them — that sailed its bosom. Then, cheerily whistling, he continued on his way.

'Really,' murmured Oakley Ashenhurst, just before he dismissed the matter from his mind, 'I must have a look at this midnight runner if he continues to frequent my block.'

So when, that midnight, again he heard the pattering footsteps in the street, young Mr. Ashenhurst was ready. Assuming that the athlete would operate upon a schedule, and that that schedule would take him past the house at midnight, the prospective Dr. Ashenhurst closed his volume of *Anatomy* at 11:55, snapped out his light, parted his window curtains, raised his window a trifle higher, and seated himself at the aperture. In the darkness, the small nickel-plated clock ticked on toward midnight. A mild breeze blew in from the street and gently stirred the curtains. Immediately opposite the house, on the other side of the street, a streetlight gleamed through dirty glass; there was no other for some distance, and the surrounding windows were as black as that of Oakley Ashenhurst, whose pipe bubbled contentedly in the darkness.

At the first rumor of the steps, he sat forward and directed his gaze outward and downward. He turned his eyes up the street toward the little park, which, however, was invisible. The middle of the street was bare, but something white was coming down the sidewalk on the near side. The slapping footsteps sounded clearly now. Lightly, evenly, with long, running strides, bounding as gracefully as an animal, the racing figure advanced out of semi-darkness into semi-light. Out of semi-light it moved into the rays of the dingy lamp. Then a cry that was a strangled scream burst from the lips of Oakley Ashenhurst, and, rising upright, he seized the curtain beside him with such haste and vigor that it tore in his grasp.

His eyes wide with horror, he saw the white figure pass below his window and enter the semi-light beyond. Inexpressibly shocked; he saw it merge from semi-light to semi-darkness, and vanish into darkness. Its pattering footsteps seemed to beat against his stunned and startled brain.

It was the nude stone statue from the fountain in the corner park.

2

And that was the sensational story I told my friend Lavender, the evening after the occurrence, as we sat in his Portland Street rooms and smoked over our coffee. It was just such a tale, I knew, as Lavender liked, for my friend Lavender, although a consulting detective of wide reputation, boasts as fantastic an imagination as I have encountered in print. He heard me through in silence, but with raised eyebrows that spoke his interest. I admit that I made the most of the incredible tale.

'Extraordinary!' he commented, when I had finished. He added at once, 'And, delightful, too! A fine theatrical touch to it. This Ashenhurst, I take it, is a sober young man?'

'Quite,' I assured him. 'I've known him only a few months, but I like him greatly. He's in one of my classes, and is an excellent student. Not at all given to romancing, I should say. He strikes me as being eminently sane and practical.'

'Yet he tells this insane story,' said Lavender, 'and, if I am to believe you, tells it with entire belief.'

'And very convincingly,' I added. 'He certainly thinks he saw something, and it has upset him.'

Lavender laughed shortly. 'No wonder,' he said. 'It would upset anybody. A very ingenious business! What do you think of it, Gilly?'

'Nothing!' I answered promptly. 'I think Ashenhurst was dreaming.'

'Nothing of the sort.'

'You don't mean to say you believe it?' I demanded. 'I knew it would please you, but I didn't expect the story to be believed.'

'I certainly don't believe he saw the statue, if that's what you mean; but he saw something very curious indeed. Now what did he see? And why did he see it? The second question is the more important of the two, and the hardest to answer.'

He smoked in silence for a moment,

thinking deeply. When he spoke, the current of his thought had changed.

'You know Ashenhurst's place?' he asked suddenly.

'I've been there once. I know the neighborhood pretty well, and I've seen the statue, so to call it. Of course, it isn't a statue; it's a figure in a fountain.'

'A distinction that doesn't help the case,' observed Lavender with a dry smile. 'Tell me about the street.'

'Well, it's called Cambridge Court, and it's only a block in length. It runs from Belden Square — which is the little park — to Crayview Avenue, which is a through street, as you know, popular with motorists. Cambridge Court is an old street, and the houses are old — once toney, but shabby-genteel now. You know the kind; every other family keeps roomers. But it's all very respectable, and the streets surrounding it are highly desirable residence thoroughfares. It's sort of hidden away, as it were, and the people who live in the court have a quiet, subdued air about them — as if the world had forgotten them, and they were glad of

11

it, if you understand what I mean.'

'Perfectly,' smiled Lavender. 'You are a bit of a poet, Gilruth. And the house?'

'Three story and attic, I think. Basement, too, probably. Brick, of course. Porcelain doorknobs. I should think it was a handsome establishment back in 1895. The front windows are bay windows, and Ashenhurst's room looks into the street from the second floor. He rents it from a family named Harden, who live in the back of the house. I think there are other roomers.'

'North side of the street? Hm-m! I think I see it. You used your eyes well on your one visit. Well, well! And Belden Square a half-block from the dwelling. The statue didn't have to run far, did it? It could leave the fountain, run around the block, and be back in no time.'

'Oh, easily!' I sarcastically agreed. 'Don't you think we ought to watch it tonight, and catch it as it steps out of the fountain?'

Lavender laughed. 'Not quite that, perhaps; but there is some watching to be done. I, for one, should like to see the thing. Shouldn't you?'

'I know Ashenhurst would like to have you,' I said.

'You've mentioned me to him, eh? Well, you guessed right when you thought I would be interested. I am interested. Something very curious is going on, Gilly, or something tremendously unimportant. I don't know which.'

'I don't follow you there.'

'I only mean that if your friend saw what he thinks he saw, the matter is most important. If he was deceived — by a resemblance, let us say — then probably the solution is very simple and unimportant. You see, there are a great many possibilities. If Ashenhurst was deceived, then he may actually have seen only some innocent idiot running off his weight, clad in a tracksuit or something of the sort. If Ashenhurst had been thinking of the statue, for any reason, and had it in his mind, he might have imagined that he saw it; in which case the solution of the matter is that Ashenhurst needs a doctor and a vacation. Or he may have seen a lunatic running naked; that certainly would heighten the resemblance to our stone friend in the park. In which case the lunatic should be apprehended, although the affair would still be relatively unimportant. But — if Ashenhurst actually saw the statue — that is, of course, somebody made up to look like the statue — the case becomes highly important, for something very significant must be back of such an impersonation; something more than just lunacy, I should say.'

'What, for instance?'

He laughed again, and ran his fingers through his thick, dark hair with a familiar gesture that brought into prominence his single plume of white.

'Well, just for instance — to frighten somebody to death! The thing certainly gave Ashenhurst a scare.'

'That's quite an idea,' I admitted, 'but you don't believe it.'

'Don't I? You don't know what I believe, Gilly — and I don't know myself yet. How should I? But you're coming with me, of course?'

'Yes,' I said promptly. 'You may gamble on that.'

He looked at his watch. 'There's three hours to midnight. I should like to have seen the statue first — out of curiosity, if nothing else — but we must assume that our friend will run again tonight, and I don't want Ashenhurst to be alone!'

Something in the earnestness of his last words arrested me, and I looked a startled inquiry. He slowly nodded.

'Yes,' he said, 'I don't know why, Gilly, but I've a notion that this may portend evil to your friend. It's just a feeling, too vague to put into logical thought, but — well, for two nights Ashenhurst didn't look out of his window, and last night he did! You see? He saw the thing, whatever it is — and it must have known that he saw it. And so, tonight — ? That's all! I can't make it any plainer.'

An unpleasant thrill ran through me, for as he spoke I had the feeling, too.

'Come on,' I cried; and got quickly to my feet. He followed more leisurely; and as we tramped down the dark stairs I added, 'We can cross the park, Jimmy, if you want a look at that thing. It's on our way.'

15

'Well — perhaps,' he agreed. 'But I should prefer not to be seen evidencing too great an interest in it.'

The night was fine, with a good moon and plenty of stars, and when our taxi had set us down not far from Belden Square, Lavender determined to have his look.

'There seems to be plenty of citizens abroad,' he argued, 'and I'll warrant there are more of them in the park. We may as well chance it.'

So, sauntering easily and ostentatiously smoking, we plunged into the little park and began our stroll diagonally across its tapestry of moonlit grass. A number of couples passed us, arm in arm, and as we approached the fountain we saw that at least a dozen persons were patrolling the paths about it. The tinkle of water sounded pleasantly in the night as it rained into the pool, and the moonlight on the stone figure of the piping faun in the midst of the falling water was memorable.

No one paid the slightest attention to us, as we idled for a moment at the stone brink; and after a careless glance or two we turned away.

'A pretty picture,' I suggested.

'Very,' said Lavender shortly. He added after an instant, 'Well, he's still there!'

In five minutes more, still easily strolling, we had entered the little street in which lived and studied my classmate, Ashenhurst.

Cambridge Court interested Lavender deeply, and his glance was everywhere as we proceeded into its dusky canyon.

'Not many lamps,' he murmured. 'Only three in the block. And the folks retire early. It can't be more than 10:30, yet nearly every house is in darkness. Two lights down there near the corner, across the street, and one here on our left. The nearest, I suppose, is Ashenhurst's?'

I corroborated the supposition, and in a moment we had turned up the steps, to discover at the top, smoking his inevitable pipe, my friend, the student. Ashenhurst's long body uncoiled and rose upright in the darkness.

'Hoped you'd come,' he said briefly, but warmly. 'This is Mr. — ?'

'Yes,' interrupted Lavender swiftly. 'Happy to know you, I'm sure. Hope the studies are coming along well. Gilly says you're an awful 'dig,' you know.'

'Come up,' said Ashenhurst abruptly, sensing a mystery, and we trudged after him up the dark stairs and into his room at the front, where he turned a puzzled face to the detective.

'It's all right, old man,' smiled Lavender, 'but your case is so peculiar that I thought it as well not to shout my name about the neighborhood. One never knows who may be listening. Nothing to add to Gilly's story, I suppose?'

The tall student shrugged, then glanced uneasily at the clock. 'Not yet,' he answered, with a rueful smile, 'Soon, maybe!'

We spoke in low tones for a time, while Ashenhurst and Lavender became acquainted, and then the conversation languished.

'It's getting along,' remarked Lavender at length, 'and it's just as well not to talk too much. I've a funny idea at the back of my head. It won't stand talking about, and it involves silence at this time. Literal silence! I may be quite wrong; but I think that from now until midnight we had better sit quite still. I'm sorry I can't be more explicit.'

I looked at him curiously in the half-darkness of the room. 'The light?' I murmured.

'Yes,' he agreed, 'let's silence the light, too.'

So Ashenhurst, no doubt vastly wondering at this strange conduct on the part of my friend, extinguished his lamp, and in darkness we began our vigil. The moments seemed to crawl as we awaited the zero hour.

From his busy smoking and an occasional restless movement, I knew that Lavender was thinking hard. My own thoughts were bewildered and incoherent, and Ashenhurst's, I fancy, were no better. What Lavender's 'funny idea' might be puzzled me profoundly; I had seen and heard all that he had seen and heard, and I was quite at sea. This, however, was the usual way of things, and I knew better than to question his decisions.

In the darkness the ticking of the little nickel-plated clock became intolerable. It seemed that hours had passed before Lavender stirred and came upright.

He moved quietly to the window, and in the poor light from the street lamp opposite, looked at his watch. I noted that he kept out of sight of the street.

'Ten minutes more,' he whispered; and again it seemed that the moments crawled.

Ashenhurst moved to my friend's side, and stood behind the curtains. I instantly followed, overpoweringly curious. Lavender drew our heads together and spoke in a sharp whisper against our ears.

'If he does not come tonight, Gilruth and I shall stay here all night. If he comes, as usual, Gilruth shall stay the night alone, and I shall go home.'

But he came — whoever he may have been.

Lavender's ears were sharp, but it was the ears of Ashenhurst that first caught the distant patter of feet, as his clutch on our arms betrayed. In a moment we all heard them, swift and terrible in the silence; and convinced as I was that the thing could not be, I felt my scalp stir.

Then the half-darkness opened, and the white figure raced past, as Ashenhurst, with a sharp breath, flung both arms about my shoulders and clung. Lavender's face was a mask set with glittering eyes. And incredible as it might be, it was the stone figure of the white faun that shot by under the window. The lamplight shone on its white clustered curls and shining shoulders, and made a glory of its body in the instant of its passing.

In the stunned silence that followed, Lavender leaped for the electric lamp on the table and snapped on the current, then leaped again for the door.

'Stay here with Ashenhurst, Gilly,' he crisply ordered. 'If there should be trouble, call me at home in an hour, or any time after that. At any rate, see me in the morning.'

A moment later we heard him plunging down the stairs on light feet, heard the street door close behind him, and from the open window saw him run off in the darkness in the direction taken by the fleeing figure.

3

The rest of the night was uneventful. In effect, we slept upon our arms, vaguely alarmed by Lavender's final remark; but no further sound disturbed the quiet of the little street, and the house itself was silent as a tomb. Not a soul, apparently, had been aroused by Lavender's departure. In the morning, not much refreshed, we both betook ourselves to Lavender's room, for Ashenhurst declared himself much too curious, not to say nervous, to think of work that day.

We discovered the detective deep in a file of *The Playbill*, borrowed from a neighboring public library reading-room. His feet were on the piano bench on which stood his typewriter, and the room was thick with tobacco fumes. He was shaved but otherwise his appearance was negligée in an extreme degree. He greeted our advent with an appraising grin.

'Had breakfast? So have I! Well,

watchmen, what of the night?'

Ashenhurst replied for us both that it had been excessively tame. 'Anything,' he added, 'would have been anti-climax after our adventure.'

'Yes,' agreed Lavender, 'destiny is frequently a bit of an artist. My own adventures ended at the same time.'

'He got away, then?' I eagerly inquired.

'Clean as a whistle! I rather expected he would. My start was a trifle late. The best I hoped for was a glimpse, but I was denied even that. The street was blank from end to end when I emerged from the house, and the boulevard was equally deserted. That, of course, is significant, eh?'

'You mean that he didn't run far? That he may have turned in some place?'

'That is one explanation. Another is that an auto was waiting for him at the corner, engine running and all ready for a quick start. That, as a matter of fact, is what I had in mind when I ran out. I thought that at least I might hear it departing. Not a sound! You may be right about his turning in some place; it's the logical assumption, for I wasn't far behind him, surely.'

'In heaven's name,' broke in Ashenhurst, 'what was it? Who was he, if it was a man?'

'I can't say, of course; but I did get an idea during the night, and it has involved all this reading without much result.' He indicated the scattered journals and smiled faintly.

'Why *The Playbill*?' I asked.

'Why not?' countered Lavender. 'The fellow is no amateur, I fancy. He ran like a professional of some kind — and jumped like a Russian dancer. Consider that, now, in connection with his amazing make-up, and there emerges somebody connected with the stage. Don't you think?'

'Um-m! Maybe!' I was not enthusiastic.

'Oh, it's a long shot, of course. But we must consider probabilities until they are shown to be improbabilities. I base my idea on more than a superficial appearance. I've been trying to guess what lies behind.'

'I lay awake guessing half the night,'

contributed Ashenhurst bitterly.

'And exactly what did you expect to find in *The Playbill*?' I insisted.

'These are old *Playbills*. The file goes back three months, and ends with last week's issue. I consider it at least possible that this ingenious fellow had been out of a job for a time. And this valuable weekly carries several columns of cards of professional gentlemen who are 'at liberty.' I'm not looking for any particular person; I'm looking for anybody who fits the description I have imagined. You see, if I am right, this fellow is not the principal in the case. What the case is, we have yet to discover; but I think this man is only a subordinate. He may not even know why he runs as he does!'

'I can't believe that, Lavender,' I demurred.

'It's very easy to believe,' he assured me. 'If for no other reason, I believe him to be a subordinate because he shows himself. If the game is important — and it's too mad not to be — the principal would not show himself so openly. He might be caught. Suppose instead of

26

waiting upstairs in Ashenhurst's room, I had been waiting for him in a passageway. I'd have had him, or seen where he went. I think the principal doesn't care whether this fellow is captured or not. He'd rather the man wouldn't be caught, of course, but it is not of great importance one way or another.'

'And this principal?' queried Ashenhurst.

'Is working elsewhere,' said Lavender.

'Elsewhere! Then why, for heaven's sake — ?'

Lavender shrugged. 'Well, well,' he said, 'I may be wrong. I'm no super-detective, Ashenhurst. It's bad business, I know, to imagine a case and then twist the facts to fit it; but I assure you it's as safe a gamble as any other method. Any way you tackle a case, you're as likely to be wrong as right.'

'But, confound it, Jimmy!' I exploded, 'why should this fellow show himself at all, in that crazy regalia?'

'Exactly,' agreed Lavender. 'Why should he? There is only one conceivable reason that holds water: he wants to be seen. If a

27

man paints himself black and parades the city between sandwich-boards, he's bound to attract attention. Obviously then, he does it in order to attract attention. But whose attention does our friend want to attract? Just as obviously, he wants to attract Ashenhurst's attention.'

'Good Lord!' exclaimed that young man. 'Well, he succeeded!'

'He did, indeed. Oh, I'm sure enough of my ground as far as I have gone. You live in Cambridge Court, and so this fellow runs in Cambridge Court. But other people live in Cambridge Court. You, however, sit up late; your window, at midnight, is the only one in the block that shows a light. There was no other light when I ran out last night, and I am sure there had not been for some time. Further, this fellow ran by four nights in a row — at least four. There may have been other, earlier nights when you didn't hear the footsteps, but on four nights anyway, he ran past your window. The first two nights you did not look out; the third night you did. He heard your exclamation, and felt sure that he had attracted

28

your attention. Last night was the test, as I read it; and last night we all looked out. And last night, he knew he had attracted you.'

'The deuce he did!'

'Yes,' I said, 'how do you know that, Jimmy?'

'Because,' said Lavender, 'I saw him look up. You fellows were excited, and were concentrating on a running statue. You didn't exactly believe in it, but the statue was in your minds — naturally. So all you saw was a running statue — an impossibility. I knew perfectly well that it was not a statue, and was determined not to be too surprised by the sight. So I watched carefully; and as he fled past he looked up at the window — just a half turn of the head as he leaped, but he looked! I saw him! And your lights were out, and my head was half-visible; I took care that it should be. Ergo, our friend believes he saw you looking out, and today he knows that he has succeeded in attracting your attention.'

'Perhaps he saw us all,' I remarked.

'I hope not,' said Lavender vigorously,

'and I think not. I kept you a trifle behind me, in deep shadow. You see, my own plans were laid.'

Ashenhurst whistled solemnly for a moment. 'And what's the next step?' he asked, at length. 'Will he run again, tonight?'

'Oh, yes, I think he will run every night until something happens.'

'What?' we demanded in the same breath.

'I don't know,' answered Jimmy Lavender.

Ashenhurst whistled again while he thought that over. 'You make me nervous,' he said finally.

'You have a right to be nervous, perhaps,' Lavender nodded. 'Although probably you are not in any serious danger. But Gilruth will stay with you every night from now until — well, until the thing happens, whatever it is — and I shall not be far away.'

There was a silence for a moment, during which Lavender looked hard at Ashenhurst. Suddenly he spoke.

'I don't want to be impertinent,

Ashenhurst, but is there any secret about you? Anything in your life that you wish to conceal? Anything somebody else would like to know?'

'Good Lord, no!' The student's reply was prompt and final.

'You don't conceal a treasure anywhere in your room, by any chance?'

Ashenhurst laughed loudly. 'Not by a large majority!'

Lavender's thoughts again revolved. Evidently something puzzled him very much. After a moment he began again.

'Do you ever go out at night?'

'Well, not very often. If you say ever, why, of course, I do, sometimes. But my exams are coming on, and I have to study pretty hard. I suppose I haven't been out after supper for weeks. I'm not much of a social climber, anyway,' finished the student with a smile.

'And you are never home during the day?'

'Never except on Sundays. I work pretty hard at the office.'

'I'll be hanged if I understand it,' declared Lavender, almost indignantly.

'My idea is a very pretty one indeed, but I can't make it work. There's something missing; something wrong. Now what the devil can it be?'

'I assure you I'm not concealing a thing,' said Ashenhurst, with some dignity.

Lavender laughed good-humoredly. 'I know you're not, old man! If you were, it would simplify things, immensely. But how about this family — what's the name? — Harden! How about the Hardens? What have they to conceal?'

'God knows,' replied Ashenhurst, mystified. 'They're as harmless an old couple as ever I met.'

'And the other roomers?'

'Same thing! Two old maids!'

'And the other floors?'

'Know 'em only by sight; but they seem all right to me. An old man and his daughter downstairs — name of Palmer. Don't know what he does. Not much of anything, I guess. Upstairs, family named Carr. They've got roomers, too — young fellow named Pomeroy, and another young fellow named Peterson. Steady workers, and go to bed early. Oh, the whole house is so respectable it's almost discouraging!'

'It does seem rather hopeless,' admitted Lavender. 'You don't happen to know who occupies the houses just beside yours? Next door, both ways?'

'Seen 'em, that's all. All respectable!'

'It's a respectable world,' said Lavender drily. 'Well, I must get to work, I suppose. I've a long day ahead of me. You fellows can do as you please, but I think you'd better separate during the day. Gilruth can join you after dark — and do it quietly, Gilly! Stay with Ashenhurst all night. I may show up before midnight, and I may not. I'll be there if I think it's necessary. And listen! Don't let our stone friend see you as he gallops past! Keep your light out — and you, Ashenhurst, stare hard out of the window. Gilruth mustn't be seen, but I want you to be seen. And neither of you are to leave the room on any account unless I tell you to.'

It sounded rather sinister, and we solemnly pledged ourselves to follow his instructions.

33

'Can't I go with you, Jimmy?' I asked, somewhat disconsolately.

'Today? It wouldn't be worth your while. Honestly, old man! A lot of tiresome inquiries, that's all. If there were any chance of danger, rest assured I'd want you right beside me.'

'I don't see what you can do,' said Ashenhurst curiously. 'You don't know which way to look, do you?'

'I'm going to look in a number of directions. I expect to talk with detectives, policemen, citizens, and heaven knows whom else. I'll be a busy young man for a time. Also, I want to make some close inquiry about a theatrical family by the name of Jordan.'

'Lavender!' I cried reproachfully. 'You've been holding out on us! You have found something!'

'Well,' he laughed, 'just an indication — no more. It's here in The Playbill, and it may not amount to a thing. You may read the notice for yourselves. On my honor, it's all I have up my sleeve.'

He selected a paper from the top of the heap and tossed it over to me, then

34

leaned across and placed a finger on a black-face 'card', halfway down a column of advertisements. Ashenhurst, greatly excited, bent over my shoulder and we read the notice together.

'Living Statuary,' ran the first line; and there followed a brief announcement that the 'Famous Jordan Family' was now at liberty and was prepared to accept engagements in vaudeville or circus.

A premonitory thrill ran along my spine, and my old newspaper instinct whispered significantly. Intuitively, I felt that Lavender was on the right track.

'You see,' he chuckled, 'there are four of them — Tom, Bert, Florence, and Lillian — all of them at liberty.'

'By heaven!' said Ashenhurst huskily, 'I believe one of them's at *large*!'

4

The day that followed was a weary one for me; possibly. for Ashenhurst, also. He solved the difficulty, however, by reporting for work, after all, some hours late, whilst I moped in the bookshops and purchased nothing. At six o'clock I joined Ashenhurst, and we supped recklessly at a favorite restaurant where I had hoped we might encounter Lavender. That ingenious person failed to appear, however, and it was with small hope of catching him at home that I called his number on the telephone. To my delight he was in his rooms; had just entered, in fact, when I rang him.

'You are a clairvoyant, Gilly,' he said. 'I was just wondering where I could catch you before you started for Ashenhurst's. Where are you now?'

I told him, adding the information that Ashenhurst was with me.

'Good,' came the familiar voice, across

the wires, 'send him home at once. He is to stay there until one or the other of us joins him. You must not be seen with him at this time. Tell him not to leave his room in any circumstances, once he gets in it. You are to meet me as soon as dark has fallen, beside the fountain in the square. Understand?'

I understood perfectly, and said so. Ashenhurst was frankly alarmed.

'He must expect trouble tonight,' he said.

'All I know is what he told me,' said I. 'You follow instructions to the letter, Ash, or you may ball up the whole show.'

'Oh, I'll behave,' he assured me, and he did, admirably.

Dusk was already settling over the city, and I calculated that if I took a streetcar I should reach the park at about the appointed time. But a wagon-load of cement very nearly ruined the program; it broke down in front of my car, and tied up traffic for an unconscionable period. When I had waited as long as I dared, I alighted and hailed a passing taxi, performing the rest of my journey in comfort. Even so, it was black dark when I entered Belden Square and hastened toward the central fountain.

Lavender, slightly impatient, awaited my coming.

'We can talk here in safety,' he remarked. 'This is about the last place any of our victims will visit tonight. The fountain, I think, has served its purpose. Tonight its counterfeit will run for the last time.'

'Great Scott!' I exclaimed, amazed. 'Is it all cleared up?'

'I know nearly everything I need to know,' said Lavender, 'except the exact 'why' of it all. That I merely suspect. But the case ends tonight, I feel certain — happily, I hope, for Ashenhurst. But he has a dangerous part to play. He seems pretty husky.'

'He's a whale of a boxer,' said I. 'Do you mean that he's likely to be assaulted?'

'Very likely, I should say. Here's the situation in a nutshell, and you must carry instructions to Ashenhurst. Jordan is the man — Bert Jordan. I'm convinced of that. That is, he's the fugitive statue!

With the aid of a theatrical friend of mine, I ran down the 'family'; and the fact is, Bert's missing! I let it be known that I wanted to hire the whole outfit for a street carnival in Aurora, and said I wanted them all to leave town tonight. Couldn't be done; they couldn't locate Bert! Tomorrow night, maybe — they weren't sure. I think they were sore at Bert, for they wanted the engagement; and I think they don't know just what he's up to. I said I'd see them again tomorrow.

'Well, Bert will run tonight, as usual, at midnight; that's a certainty. That's where Ashenhurst comes in. I'll see him before he starts, but you must prepare him. The minute he sees Jordan coming, he is to leave the room, run downstairs after him, and follow him down the street. I think Jordan will give battle, and Ashenhurst must be prepared to defend himself. Jordan may be very ugly. Anyway, there'll be a couple of plain-clothes men hidden away nearby, and at the proper moment they'll nab Jordan. If possible, though, I want to know where he goes, for I think he turns in some place in the block, as you once suggested.'

'Where will you be all this time?' I pertinently asked, for by now it was obvious that Lavender's role was to be cast elsewhere.

'I'll be in Ashenhurst's rooms, and so will you. You go to Ashenhurst now, with my instructions. Get into the house quietly; it may be watched. We've worked so quickly, though, that I think we have aroused no suspicion. I'll follow you in a little while, and I, too, must get in without being seen. I could tell you all this later, I suppose; but it may be close to midnight before I can risk entering the house.'

'One question, Jimmy,' I said. 'Why is Ashenhurst to run out while we stay behind in the room?'

'Well,' smiled Lavender grimly, 'I want it to be supposed that when Ashenhurst runs out, his room is empty.'

'Oh!' I said, suddenly enlightened. 'The principal — '

'Is the man I want. Exactly!'

'I see — I think I do! Then the statue — Jordan — was to attract attention?'

'Quite so, and to draw Ashenhurst from his room. That was the ultimate design. It might never have worked, or it might have worked wrong — as it did, by Jove! — but that was the plan. If it had failed, I suppose some other plan would have been worked out.'

'And what is in Ashenhurst's room?'

'Hanged if I know,' said Lavender. 'Whatever it is, somebody wants it pretty badly, don't you think? And I know, at last, who Mr. Somebody is. I'll introduce you to him in a little while. Now hurry along, and don't be seen entering the house. And not a sound, after you have entered, from either of you!'

Well, the affair was getting warm! And something told me that we were all in for a lively evening.

I left the park in leisurely fashion, and plunged into the inky depths of Cambridge Court. Not a soul was in the block as far as could be seen. The trio of sickly streetlamps, long distances apart, blinked sadly in the blackness. I passed the first one hastily; the next was in the center of the block opposite Ashenhurst's room, but on the far side of the street. I approached cautiously, but without ostentatious secrecy, and quietly climbed the stairs of the objective dwelling. The door was unlocked, and I entered without ceremony, climbing stairs again to Ashenhurst's room so softly that when I had closed his door behind me the student had his first knowledge of my approach.

The room, as usual, was in darkness save for the blaze of light from the electric lamp upon the table. This gleamed on one wall, and was faintly reflected on the window; but the corners of the room were black. I motioned Ashenhurst to silence, and whispered his instructions. He nodded understandingly — relieved, I think, that shortly the whole matter would be ended. A glance at the clock showed three hours before midnight, and another intolerable wait was before us.

At ten o'clock, Ashenhurst snapped off his light at the switch, and the remainder of the vigil was kept in darkness. At eleven, the door creaked gently, and through the blackness Jimmy Lavender came to our side.

'All well,' he whispered. 'Our men are placed, and there ought to be no hitch. You understand your part, Ashenhurst?'

'Every comma,' said the long student, in the same tone, 'except this damned silence, Mr. Lavender. It gets on my nerves.'

'Sorry,' Lavender whispered back, 'but it can't be helped. The danger is from within the house. I thought you had guessed that. You may smoke if you like.'

We felt better when we had all lighted cigars. The room seemed less black, the silence less profound. So another hour passed away and midnight was upon us.

'Ready!' murmured Lavender. 'Stand by the window, Ashenhurst; let yourself be seen. When he passes, rush for the door, with some noise, and downstairs after him. Don't upset the neighborhood, but don't be afraid of a little noise. I want it perfectly evident that you are leaving the house.'

Ashenhurst followed instructions without an error. The stone faun held no terror for any of us now, and the patter of racing feet in the outside darkness only told us that the moment for action had come. Ashenhurst, leaning far out of the window, cried out once as the white figure shot past, then jumped for the door and pelted down the stairs in the darkness. I moved toward the window, but Lavender's hand restrained me.

'Careful!' he sharply whispered. 'The trouble begins now — and I don't know where it will come from!'

Almost as he spoke, there sounded beyond the door a light thudding of feet; then the door creaked and swung inward and a long beam of white light cut a ribbony path across the carpet. It was followed by the dark figure of a man, holding an electric torch, who, with a swift lithe bound, sprang to a corner of the room and stooped to the boards. It had all happened so quickly that for a moment I was breathless; then as I was about to spring upon the intruder, Lavender's restraining hand again fell upon my arm. There followed a moment of tense and painful silence, then a crackling sound as of splintering wood, and the heavy breathing of the man in the corner. He was working furiously in the patch of light thrown by his torch, and once, as he half-turned, the gleam fell across a hard, seamed face and an eye that glittered like that of a madman. Save for his asthmatic breathing, and the occasional crackling of wood, the room was heavy with silence.

Our time had come. Lavender's hand was taken from my arm. Then his voice, swift and hard, and icy as a mountain stream, cut through the chamber.

'Hands up, Wilcox! Quick!' And to me, 'Lights, Gilly!'

But as I sprang for the electric lamp, the intruder, ignoring the command and the leveled revolver which he knew lay back of it, flung himself forward in the darkness in the direction of Lavender's voice. Instantly, I, too, jumped into action, and more by luck than design, blundered at once into the man called Wilcox. In an instant the fight of my life was on.

We met with a shock that was terrific, and clung like tigers. The fellow had a grasp like an animal; against it my own proved powerless. A chair crashed over, and we began to whirl. We whirled until I thought my wits were deserting me. Up and down the room we thrashed, colliding with everything, unmindful of bumps and bruises; and all without a sound from either of us. Inextricably mixed as we were, Lavender could do nothing but encourage me with his voice. My hands tried desperately to work themselves upward to the throat of the man who was crushing me, but I was a child in his grasp. The constant pressure and the wild, whirling waltz had stolen my breath. I felt myself slipping — giving.

At that instant, Lavender, who had discovered the lights, out at the switch, flooded the room with light from every bulb; and at the same instant we crashed into the center table. The impact broke my opponent's grasp; he sprang back, then leaped for the door. Two seconds later the fight was over, and the man called Wilcox was helpless on the floor. Lavender, cool and collected, had greeted the fellow's spring with a straight right, shot forward with all the force of the trained back and loins that lay behind it. The blow was terrific, and the man dropped as if he had been pole-axed.

Lavender stooped and studied the hard face for a moment, almost with pity. Then I heard the clink of handcuffs, and with a little shrug my friend rose to his feet.

'Bernard Wilcox,' he said laconically. 'Paroled convict — used to occupy this room. Planted his loot here and went to jail. Came back for it tonight.'

He added with a grin, 'R. I. P.' Then lighted a cigar and dropped into a chair to await the coming of Ashenhurst.

5

Twenty minutes later, Mr. Oakley Ashenhurst, wearing a highly decorative black
eye and a wide smile, tramped upstairs at
the head of an extraordinary procession.
After him there entered the room two
husky detectives, half-carrying between
them what had once been the celebrated
Bert Jordan of the 'Famous Jordan
Family', and behind them stalked a tall,
uniformed officer in whom I recognized
Captain D'Arcy of the Lincoln Park
station. Bringing up the rear was a motley
of half-gowned, bathrobed citizens and
citizenesses, among whom were the
shrinking figures of old Mr. and Mrs.
Harden and the two other roomers,
elderly women with their hair in curl-
papers. It was a sight to move the gods to
laughter, and Lavender and I, being
essentially human, lay back and laughed.
D'Arcy, too, wore a broad grin.

'Got him, I see,' said the police captain,

with a nod to the prostrate Wilcox. He stooped over the man on the floor. 'Yep, it's Wilcox!'

Bernard Wilcox, who had recovered his senses, glowered back with evil eyes.

'And you, I see, have Jordan,' said Lavender pleasantly. 'The others, I suppose, escaped?'

'Yes,' answered D'Arcy with a frown. 'Big auto all ready to pick up Jordan, over in the next block. He had to run through a passage to get to it, and they may have seen us nail Jordan in the passage; I don't know. Anyway, all we saw when we got over there was a trail of dust and sound.'

'Unimportant,' said Lavender, 'although you'll probably get them through Jordan. Our statue doesn't seem as lively a cricket as he was a little while ago.'

All eyes were turned back to the amazing figure of Bert Jordan of the 'Famous Jordan Family'. He was an astonishing spectacle. From neck to ankle he was encased in dull white fleshings, above which his white, painted face, like that of a clown, now registered profound depression. His hair, elaborately whitened and held in place by a white net, had been curled in neat horns on his brow and temples, but at the moment it was much disordered. On his feet were white gloves of the sort worn by fashionable bathers in the sands of expensive bathing beaches. But the celebrated Bert Jordan had lost much of his 'white' in his tussle with Ashenhurst and the police, and he now presented a very lugubrious appearance. I felt sorry for the fellow, and I think Lavender did, too.

'Want to talk, Jordan?' inquired Lavender. 'Might as well, you know.'

Jordan grinned sheepishly. 'Sure, I'll talk,' he said, 'What d'ya want to know?'

'What did you soak Mr. Ashenhurst for?'

'Dough!' replied Mr. Jordan promptly. 'Plenty of dough!'

'So I should imagine. Mr. Wilcox foot the bill?'

'Whatever his name is,' said Jordan.

'He's a liar!' asserted Wilcox, from the floor, with a string of oaths.

'Well, I'll talk,' said Lavender. 'I'm not a liar. There are some things I want to know. You were out of a job, Jordan, and you met this fellow Wilcox. He offered you a job. Good money in it. You fell for it. But how did you happen to run across Wilcox?'

'Met him in the park up here, one day — near that damn fountain!'

'I see! Of course, that would do it. I ought to have thought of that. Did you know Wilcox before that?'

'He used to be in a circus where I was,' said Jordan, 'but his name wasn't Wilcox then. It was Brown.'

'You're a liar!' declared Wilcox savagely.

'Hm-m!' grunted Lavender, 'That pretty nearly tells me all I need to know. The statue, of course, suggested this crazy scheme to get Ashenhurst out of his room some night. Wilcox knew you were in the statue line, as it were, and so was born the great idea. He suggested it, of course?'

'Sure,' said Jordan. 'He said he wanted to get some guy's goat, and when the guy ran out at me, I was to beat him up, toss him into the auto and take him off somewhere overnight.'

'You had no objections, I suppose?'

'Well,' hedged the circus performer, 'I was pretty broke, and I needed the dough. But I didn't like his damn fool scheme. I told him I'd go up and drag the guy out, if he wanted me to; or throw stones at his window until he chased me. I didn't want to dress up. It seemed kinda foolish to me.'

'Quite right,' smiled Lavender. 'And what do you think of Wilcox — or Brown — now, Mr. Jordan?'

Jordan looked suddenly significant. He turned his eyes on the recumbent Wilcox, almost stealthily. Then he looked at the police captain, and finally back at Lavender. After these elaborate preparations, he raised his forefinger and touched his temple, where a white curl now hung limply.

'I think he's coo-coo!' he said.

'Excellent,' said Lavender. 'So do I! I think, Captain, we shall have to make things as easy as possible for Mr. Jordan, who is, after all, only an erring person of temperament. If your men will remove both of these gentlemen now, we'll let these good folks go to bed, and I'll have a chat with you about this case.'

When the prisoners had been removed, and the oaths of Bernard Wilcox had died away in the distance, Lavender resumed his tale.

'Jordan is perfectly right, of course,' he said. 'Wilcox is a bit touched. Nobody but a lunatic would have suggested such a scheme to get a man out of his room. The meeting with Jordan gave him the idea, no doubt; that and the proximity. of the statue.'

He turned suddenly to Mrs. Harden, whose attire now had been augmented by a huge shawl.

'Did you recognize this man Wilcox, Mrs. Harden?' he asked.

'Yes, sir, I did! He's the man upstairs they call Pomeroy!'

'Pomeroy, eh? It had to be either Pomeroy or Peterson. I wasn't able to see either of them, and so I couldn't be sure. You see, Gilly, five years ago, before Mrs. Harden had this flat, this Wilcox-or Pomeroy — or Brown — or whatever his real name is — occupied the room now occupied by our friend Ashenhurst. He roomed with a very decent family named Dickson, but he himself was a clever thief. In time, he was caught and sent to Joliet for a stretch. He had planted some of his loot in this room, however; when, not long ago, he was released on parole, he came back here to get it. He couldn't get the same room, but he was lucky enough to get a room upstairs, and there he laid his plans to get down here and recover the stuff he had planted.

'I suppose he did a lot of thinking about it, while he was tucked away down in Joliet, and after a while he became — shall we say, a bit obsessed? Once located upstairs — he had a room at the back, I believe — his problem was to get into Ashenhurst's room some time when Ashenhurst was out. It would seem at first glance to be an easy enough problem, but as it turned out it was a hard one. For one reason and another, he couldn't gain access, and, finally he hit upon this mad scheme to force Ashenhurst out. I saw D'Arcy today, and he was able to give me some information that fitted in with my preconceived idea of things.

'It was obvious from the first that Jordan's amazing performance was to draw attention to himself, and after a bit it became equally obvious that he was trying to lure Ashenhurst from the house. But why? So that he, or somebody else, could get into Ashenhurst's room. I preferred to believe it was somebody else — that Jordan was only a subordinate. This turned, out to be correct, for Jordan now has no idea what Wilcox wanted in this room. It was necessary to find a trace of somebody who for some years had been absent from society, who had occupied this room — at least, this house. D'Arcy remembered a number of men who might answer, among them Wilcox. I looked them all up in the police records, and Wilcox was the man. Under that name he had once been known to live at this address. He had lived here at the time he was sent to Joliet. And when I learned that recently he had been paroled, the whole case was clear. I knew that Bernard Wilcox was somewhere in or near this house, and that Jordan was his agent. I'm hanged if I know whether Wilcox's scheme to draw Ashenhurst out was a stupid one or a very clever one. Its very madness bothered me, and kept me from guessing the motive earlier than I did.'

D'Arcy, who had listened with many approving nods, now cleared his throat.

'And exactly what did Wilcox want here?' he asked. 'Where is this loot, Lavender?'

Lavender rose to his feet and strode over to the corner of the room in which the convict had been at work.

'It is under this splintered board,' he said. 'As you represent authority here tonight, suppose you investigate.'

The police captain was beside him at a bound. 'By jigger!' he exclaimed, and fell furiously to work.

With a resounding crack the board at length came up — and neatly packed beneath it, in the narrow groove, lay little packages of bills and papers, and a bag of jewels, that cleared the mystery of a dozen unsolved robberies.

When the captain, with many eulogies

and handclasps, had departed with his treasure, I turned with a broad grin to Jimmy Lavender, and found him grinning at me. The Hardens, who still remained, looked mystified, and Ashenhurst alternately puffed at his cigar and stroked his battered eye.

'There is one question, Jimmy,' I began; but he took the words away from me.

'That you don't find an answer to! Neither do I! Gilly, and you, Ashenhurst, and you, too, Mr. and Mrs. Andrew Harden — you have seen me turn over two prisoners and a young fortune to the police. You have seen me do things that no doubt appear very clever. Yes, I am a very clever young man! And from first to last there has been one thing I didn't know, and don't know now. It has bothered me more than any one detail I have ever encountered; and there seems to be no answer. This case is ended — the men are locked up, or will be shortly — and I know that my reasoning throughout has been accurate and justified. But I'm hanged if I'm not still bothered by that one question. Tell them what it is, Gilly!'

'Why didn't Wilcox get in during the day when Ashenhurst was at work? Why did he wait until night when he knew Ashenhurst would be at home?'

'There you have it!' agreed Lavender. 'Why — exactly why? It was the obvious thing for him to do, the simplest thing to do, one would think. I have no doubt at all that he tried it and failed — but why? In the morning, no doubt, he would be likely to encounter Mrs. Harden on her cleaning-up expedition; but the afternoons were safe. He had a clear field. From at least one o'clock until five, the house would be practically deserted, and this room would be empty as Mother Hubbard's cupboard. Why didn't he, Ashenhurst?'

A queer clucking noise sounded suddenly from the throat of Mrs. Harden. Her lips were working frantically. It was difficult to say whether she was about to laugh or weep. Lavender gazed upon her with growing suspicion.

'Why, why — ' she stammered, 'the fact

is, Mr. Ashenhurst — I didn't think there would be any harm in it. I'm getting a bit old — and your bed is the best in the house, you know! I was sure you wouldn't mind — The fact is, Mr. Ashenhurst, I always came in here for a bit of a nap in the afternoon — right after dinner — and slept till Mr. Harden came in at half-past five. I'm sure — '

But if she ever finished her embarrassed speech, I did not hear the end, for in the midst of it Lavender, with a joyous roar, flung himself across the bed in question and laughed until he cried.

The Taggert Case

1

I had not seen my friend Lavender for some days, and through no fault of my own. He was out of town. But faithfully every morning I strolled around to his rooms, collected his mail, and tried to imagine that in the absence of the great Lavender I was myself a person of importance. I even opened letters that appeared to be significant and, when necessary, replied with tidings of my friend's absence; but throughout the week of silence that followed his departure there had been nothing warranting a wire to him in Wisconsin, where I knew he was engaged upon a will case of national prominence.

On the eighth day of my voluntary factotumship, I sauntered toward the dingy edifice whose upper story concealed the curious activities of my remarkable friend.

I suppose there were not a dozen men

in the community who knew Lavender to be a detective, but the regular postman was one of these, and this friendly individual I met as I entered Portland Street.

'Well, I see he's home,' he cheerfully greeted me.

'The deuce he is!' I exclaimed.

'Yep, saw him this morning on my first trip. I've got a letter for him. You going up?'

'Yes;' I said indignantly, 'and he's going to be called down! He might have let a fellow know when he was coming.'

The man in gray laughed. 'Now you see him and now you don't,' he chanted, and fished in his sack until he had found the single letter intended for James Eliot Lavender.

But I withheld the bitterly affectionate greeting that lay upon my lips as I burst into the library, for I quickly saw that Lavender was not alone. He was deep in consultation with one of the most striking young women I had ever seen. Both looked up at my noisy entrance.

'Hello, Gilly,' said my friend casually. 'I

was about to telephone you. Glad to see you! Let me make you acquainted with Miss Dale Valentine. My friend Mr. Gilruth, Miss Valentine.'

I bowed and stared. We had had young lady visitors before, but seldom such arresting specimens as this one. And her name and face were curiously familiar, although at the moment I could not place her.

'You are wondering where you have seen Miss Valentine before, no doubt Probably you have noticed her portrait in the newspapers. Her engagement recently was announced by the press. Draw up a chair, Gilly, and listen to what Miss Valentine will tell you. Do you mind repeating the story?' he asked his client, with a friendly smile. 'Mr. Gilruth is my assistant and will work with me in this matter.'

Of course, I knew her as soon as he spoke about the newspapers. She was the season's bright and particular 'bud', and her approaching marriage to a young man of her own set had filled the society columns. What in the world, I wondered, could this darkly beautiful girl, with a woman's greatest happiness less than a week away as I remembered it, want with my friend Lavender?

'Something very strange has happened, Mr. Gilruth,' she said frankly. 'Perhaps something very terrible.' Her lips trembled, and she paused as if to control an emotion that threatened to destroy her calm. 'My fiancé, Mr. Parris, is missing. That is everything, in a word. He — '

Noting her distress, Lavender hastily threw himself into the breach.

'Yes,' he said, 'that is the whole story. In a word, Mr. Rupert Parris has disappeared, practically on the eve of his wedding. Miss Valentine cannot explain so remarkable an action by any ordinary reason, and quite naturally she suspects that something may have happened to Mr. Parris; that he may have been injured, or abducted, or even — possibly — killed; although, as I tell her, that seems, unlikely in the circumstances. There is no one else to ask that a search be made — Mr. Parris is alone in the world — and Miss Valentine has determined to risk the unpleasantness of possible gossip and ask for investigation. The case is to be kept from the newspapers if humanly possible, but one way or another Mr. Parris is to be found. Miss Valentine has honored us by asking us to conduct the search.'

The young woman nodded her head gratefully in acknowledgment of his understanding and his delicate statement of the facts.

'Today is Tuesday,' continued my friend, 'and Mr. Parris has been missing only since Sunday evening, so it is possible that he may appear at any moment with a quite reasonable explanation of his absence. Something of the highest importance to him may have occurred which called him away without giving him opportunity to notify Miss Valentine. We dare not assume that, however, for it is also possible that Mr. Parris is at this moment in need of our assistance. Now, Miss Valentine, your fiancé called you on the telephone on Sunday evening — ?'

'Shortly after six o'clock,' she took up the story as he paused. 'He said that he had just dined, and that he would be over within an hour. I waited, and — he did not come. I supposed that something unexpected had detained him, but when he had not arrived at nine o'clock I became anxious and called his rooms. He was not there and had not been in all evening. Nor had he been seen at his club. There was no further word from him that evening, and there has been none since. I am at my wit's end, and — '

'Quite so,' interrupted Lavender, smiling, 'but we are not, Miss Valentine. So far as it is possible, you will please let us do the worrying from now on.' His engaging smile conjured a feeble response. 'You had not planned to go out on Sunday evening?'

'No, we were to spend the evening at home — at my home, of course. Dad was there, and he was very fond of Rupert. They always played a game of chess when Rupert came.'

'Your mother, I think, is dead?'

'Yes.'

'And how long had you known Mr. Parris, Miss Valentine?'

'For about a year. We have been engaged for about three months. The engagement was to have been short. Mr. Parris and my father were both opposed to long engagements.' She paused, then continued: 'Perhaps I should tell you that it was largely on my father's account — for his sake, rather — that Mr. Parris and I became engaged. Dad liked him very much, and when I had come to know him I liked him, too. My father naturally wanted me to marry happily, and he had a high opinion of Mr. Parris, who is somewhat older than I. Do not misunderstand me, please! Of course, I was very much distressed by his disappearance, and I shall do everything in my power to find him. I think I have proved that.'

'I see. Will you describe Mr. Parris for us?'

'He is of middle height, and quite slim; dark hair worn rather longer than usual. Complexion somewhat pale. He was forty-one on his last birthday. I suppose he would be called good-looking.'

'You can give us a photograph, of course?'

'I'm sorry, but I can't. Rupert was averse to having his photograph taken, and I haven't one in the house.'

Lavender frowned and nodded. He drummed his fingers on his chair-arm for a moment.

'Gilly,' he suddenly said to me, 'you must trace that telephone call. Miss Valentine will — '

'You mean Rupert's — Mr. Parris's call to me?' asked Miss Valentine quickly. Then she blushed. 'I did that, Mr. Lavender!'

'Good for you!' cried Lavender. 'I ought to have asked you.'

'Yes,' she continued, 'when he didn't come, I didn't know what to think, and when I had called his rooms and his club, and no one knew anything about him, I was afraid, and I — I was ashamed to do it — but I traced his call.'

'Admirable!' my friend exclaimed. 'The most sensible thing you could have done. Where did it come from?'

'That is strange, too, and I can't quite

believe it. Perhaps the operator made a mistake and traced the wrong call; but I was told that it had come from the office of the *Morning Beacon!*'

'A newspaper office,' I said quickly. 'Then we have another clue.'

'No,' she said, with a shake of her head, 'for when I called the *Beacon,* as I did, nobody ever had heard of Mr. Parris. I had to be very careful, you see, for if I hinted at his disappearance there would have been a dreadful story about it the next morning. I didn't identify him for them; I just asked for a Mr. Parris who had telephoned from there; but there was no such man in the office, they said, and had not been. When they became curious I thanked them and rang off.'

'Odd,' muttered Lavender, 'very odd!' He sat with creased brow for a moment, then leaped to his feet. 'No matter, Miss Valentine! We'll begin at once. I hope before long we shall have a happy report for you.'

The dark young woman stood up and extended her hand. There was embarrassment in her eyes.

'You know,' she faltered, 'the wedding date is — set? It is to be — '

'I know,' said Lavender, understanding her hesitation. 'It is set for a week from tomorrow. You mean that if there is to be a wedding, and no gossip, I must work quickly. Believe me, Miss Valentine, I shall!'

'Thank you,' she said simply, 'I know you will.'

Then with a quick grip of my hand, and a bright, brave look at us both, she was gone. Lavender looked after her thoughtfully.

'A fine girl,' said my friend at length. 'If this Parris has jilted her and run away for any reason, I'll — well, I'll make him regret it, Gilly, if he's living!'

'You think that is the case?' I asked.

'It is the obvious answer to the riddle,' he replied. 'But certainly I have no right to think it. In fact, I don't think it as vigorously as I may have suggested it — but it must be considered. After all, the poor devil may be dead, or even — as she suggested — a prisoner somewhere, although it doesn't look much like abduction. Full grown men are abducted on their wedding eves only in books.'

I plunged my hand into my pocket. 'By George, Lavender,' I exclaimed, handing him the letter the postman had given me, 'this was handed me outside the house, and I clean forgot it! And talk about the long arm of coincidence! Look at that return address!'

He received the envelope from my hand and read the printed card in its corner. As plain as print could make it, the inscription invited a return in five days to the *Morning Beacon!*

'Coincidence?' he asked, looking up with a quizzical smile. 'I wonder! The *Beacon* was suspicious when Miss Valentine called up, remember.'

He tore open the envelope and a card dropped out. There was nothing else. Lavender picked the card from the floor.

'As usual, the plot begins to thicken,' he continued, chuckling. 'If this is coincidence, it's a striking case of it.'

The card bore the engraved name 'Mr. Gorman B. Taggart,' and underneath in pencil script, '2:30 p.m.'

'Taggart!' I cried.

'Yes,' said Lavender, 'Taggart! Owner and publisher of the *Morning Beacon*. And he will be here, if I do not misread his laconic message, at 2:30 by his expensive gold watch.' He produced his own, and frowned.

'It's after 2:30 now,' I contributed uselessly.

'Yes, confound it!' agreed my friend. 'I hope he didn't see Miss Valentine leaving this house! I have a feeling, Gilly, that a curious muddle is developing. There's the bell now, and in a moment you will see my feeling verified, when Gorman B. Taggart stands upon my rug and tells us the meaning of his visit.'

He walked across to the door and flung it open, and through the aperture there shortly entered the mountainous and well-known figure of the famous newspaper proprietor; thereafter for twenty minutes it occupied a creaking armchair by the window.

'Your secretary?' queried Taggart, in a bass rumble. His glance was upon me.

'My assistant,' corrected Lavender

politely. 'What can we do for you, Mr. Taggart?'

'Damn it!' said Gorman B. Taggart, 'I hope you can do a great deal.' He frowned at us both for an instant, then continued: 'Mr. Lavender, my circulation manager, Moss Lennard, has been with me for forty years without missing a day, and now I'm afraid something has happened to the old man. He's been missing since Sunday evening!'

2

We found our pipes soothing after our second visitor had gone away. Lavender looked questioningly at me, and I looked back at him without a glimmer of light in my brain.

'Muddle is right!' I said at length. 'You guessed it, Jimmy!'

He laughed a little.

'And yet it may clear things amazingly,' he retorted. 'That there is a connection between the two I have not the slightest doubt. On the face of things, I would say that they are together, wherever they are — Parris and Lennard. If Taggart's story is correct — and I must suppose that it is — they must have disappeared at about the same time; and note how easily a theory may be constructed that will fit the case. Parris called Miss Valentine shortly after six; that call, traced, is found to have originated in the *Beacon* office.

'Now for Lennard: after being seen

around the place all afternoon — Sunday is a working day for a morning newspaper — he goes out to dinner about half past six and does not return. Lennard is a familiar figure in the *Beacon* neighborhood, and he was actually seen in conversation with a man, who may very well have been Parris, outside the office; that is what the cigar dealer next door told Taggart. The cigar man knew Lennard, but of course he did not know Parris. Parris could have made his call from any one of a dozen phones in the *Beacon* office without being seen — of course, with the connivance of Lennard.

'Our first theory, then, would shape up about like this: Parris, for reasons of his own, as yet unknown, goes to see old Lennard at the *Beacon* office, and — obviously — discharges at him some revelation that alarms the older man. Whatever it is, it is important enough to make both seek safety in flight. Of course, it follows that they have known each other for some time. We shall have to look into the past of both these gentlemen before we are through; meanwhile, instead of one man we have two to look for, and our task is simplified because by finding one we at least get word of the other.

'We shall have to proceed carefully, for we can't let Taggart suspect that we are looking for any one other than Lennard. For Taggart we are running down only Moss Lennard, for Miss Valentine we are seeking Rupert Parris; two cases ostensibly; yet we know that we are working the same case. Really, it begins to look very promising.'

'I'm glad you think so, Lavender,' I said dryly. 'To me it looks like a bigger job than ever. Two missing men — twice as much work.'

'No, half as much,' he corrected. 'Our description of Parris might be better; as it stands, it will fit hundreds of fellows of his class. We are better off with Lennard. Taggart's description is clear enough, and here is the photograph he left. Well-preserved old chap, isn't he? I'll have a copy made for you, and you can carry it around with you. I've an idea that we shall find Moss Lennard before we find Rupert Parris. And now for an important question: Did these two skip together, or did they separate?'

'If they are seeking safety from something, they probably separated,' I promptly answered.

'You may be right. That is what they should have done, of course. Well, our first step must be to visit the haunts of each. Parris lived at the Sheridan Arms, and belonged to the November Club. Lennard, Taggart said, is an old bachelor, and has three rooms in a private house on the West Side. We may as well work together, at first anyway, for it's little we'll learn at the Sheridan, and we can proceed almost at once to Lennard's place.'

We taxied to the Sheridan Arms and learned exactly what Lavender had expected — nothing, or practically nothing, that we did not already know. Parris had not been seen at the hotel on the Sunday of his disappearance and had not called up. Nobody thought anything of this, because Parris was not often seen at the hotel, anyway; he maintained a room for his occasional convenience and was supposed to spend his time at the club. There was nothing in his room to suggest that he had left it permanently; indeed there was much to suggest that he would certainly return — expensive garments, pipes, knickknacks, a pigskin suitcase, and the usual impedimenta of a bachelor's chamber, including a handsome photograph of Miss Dale Valentine in a silver frame.

A chat with the switchboard operator gave us our single fact of interest, and that merely added weight to our already acquired knowledge. The girl testified that several times in recent weeks Parris — who was well-known to her by sight — had telephoned to the *Beacon* office, and each time she had heard him ask for Mr. Lennard. She had never overheard any conversation between the two, however, and Parris had never stayed long in the booth.

'At least,' said Lavender, 'we have established a connection between them.'

At the November Club little more was to be learned. Parris was not often on hand; at any rate, he was seldom seen in the lounge; and although he had a room, it was not much occupied. He came and went without question, and it was not always known when he was in the place and when he was not. He did not court publicity, and to us it was apparent that for reasons of his own he must divide his time between the hotel and the club, so far as sleeping was concerned.

'A queer bird, this Parris,' commented Lavender, as we left the last place. He looked at his watch. 'Now, Gilly, if we haven't lost Lennard's address, we should be able to get out there and back before dinner time. Remember we are to dine with the great Gorman B. Taggart at his club, and although he may be five minutes late for an appointment, we may not.'

Moss Lennard, circulation manager of the *Beacon* for many, years, lived far out on West Jackson Boulevard, but our taxi deposited us before his door in a little time; and here for the first time we received a scrap of highly important information. Although Taggart certainly had caused inquiries to be made at Lennard's rooms, apparently they had

81

been of a perfunctory character, and no doubt by telephone, for the housekeeper was able to tell us at once that Lennard had gone to Milwaukee.

'Yes, sir,' said the elderly female, with a series of nods, 'Mr. Lennard went up to Milwaukee by the night boat, sir, on Sunday. That is, he told me he was going to Milwaukee, sir, and by the night boat, and so I suppose that is what he did. Didn't say when he would be back, sir, and naturally I didn't ask him. 'Twasn't my business, and Mr. Lennard is not a boy, sir. He's a man that knows very well how to take care of himself. He's been here, off and on, for a good many years, and we never worried when he was away.'

'He was away a good deal?' asked Lavender.

'No doubt,' replied our garrulous informant. 'Yes, I suppose he was. Him being a newspaper man, sir, he was often away on duty for days at a time. Sometimes he stayed at the office; sometimes he was out of town; sometimes he was here. We never bothered about Mr. Lennard. And on Sunday morning he said to me, 'Mrs. Barrett' — that being my name, sir — I'm going up to Milwaukee tonight by the night boat. I don't feel well, Mrs. Barrett,' he said, 'and a lake trip is what I need, and it's little time I get during the day for boats,' he said. And so he went, and if he is not back at his office, then you may be sure he's stayed in Milwaukee. Never fear, sir, about Mr. Lennard.'

'Quite so,' said Lavender, who had followed this long speech with polite attention, 'but it seems strange, nevertheless, Mrs. Barrett, that he did not notify his office that he was going; and it is stranger still that, finding he could not get back the next day, he did not wire. I represent Mr. Taggart, as I have told you, and he is anxious about Mr. Lennard. He asked me to look, into Mr. Lennard's rooms while I was here, to see if Mr. Lennard had left a note maybe, or something of the sort — possibly, an address in Milwaukee, eh?'

The old woman sniffed.

'It's a strange time for Mr. Taggart to be anxious,' she asserted scornfully, 'and him paying Mr. Lennard a salary which he should be ashamed to give a man after forty years! Many's the time I've heard Mr. Lennard say that he wouldn't stand it much longer, no he wouldn't. He could get more money on any other paper, he said, and it was only loyalty that kept him to the *Morning Beacon*. Yes, sir, loyalty is what it was! He'd been with 'em from a lad. And now because he takes a little trip to Milwaukee — '

'Was Mr. Lennard a drinking man?' interrupted Lavender with a smile, edging past her into the hall.

'Well, sir, he certainly was that, sometimes, but never a rough word from him, or a sound out of his room. He drank his liquor, sir, like a gentleman. Yes, sir, you can see his rooms; as neat and clean as a pin they are — '

Still mumbling she turned away, and we followed her into the dark hallway and up a flight of stairs to the second storey, where she opened a door and asked us to enter. When she had pushed an electric button we looked around us upon a comfortable sitting room, every detail of which bore out her claims as to its neatness. But Lavender's interest at once was centered upon an old desk that stood beside the front window. He crossed to it, with only a hasty glance at the bedroom, which opened off the sitting room.

'This, I suppose, is his desk? Very interesting indeed! And as you say, Mrs. Barrett, not an empty bottle about the place.' He winked at me. 'A fine gentleman, this Mr. Lennard. I can see. Well now, about that Milwaukee address — ' And he began to rummage with a practiced hand in the drawers of the old desk.

His search was unrewarded by anything of value, and he turned his attention to the wastebasket, still half full of old papers, while I explored the bedroom. When I returned, Lavender, with a gleam in his eye, was saying goodbye to the housekeeper. It occurred to me that he had found something. At any rate, he was pressing a coin into the old lady's willing palm.

'Thank you very much,' I heard him say. 'Come on, Gilly, we must get along or we shall be late for dinner. By the way,

Mrs. Barrett, did Mr. Lennard ever make any trips home?'

'Home?' echoed our humble servant. 'You mean to Washburn? Well, yes, sir, but not very often. Only twice that I can remember while he's been here. But I've often heard him speak of his old home. That's where he was born.'

'Of course,' said Lavender. 'Washburn, Indiana, isn't it?'

'No, sir,. Washburn, Illinois. Right here in our own state. Mr. Lennard is one of our great men, sir, like Lincoln and Grant and Logan — '

'And Roosevelt,' interrupted Lavender wickedly. 'Well, that is very interesting. Thank you very much.'

And after a time we were out in the street and in the waiting taxicab.

'What were you getting at?' I demanded, as we started.

'Nothing in particular,' smiled my friend, 'but we'll have to investigate Lennard's past sooner or later, and I just wanted to find out where he originated. She's certainly a loquacious old person, isn't she? I'll have to have another talk

86

with her some time. No, Gilly, I got what I really wanted out of the wastebasket.'

I jumped. 'You mean that you got something you went there expecting to find?'

'I went there hoping to find a correspondence between Parris and Lennard,' he replied, 'and what do you suppose I discovered?' He fumbled in his pocket, and produced an electric torch, for dusk was now falling and the interior of the taxicab was almost dark. 'This!' he concluded triumphantly, and turned his light on a crumpled sheet of paper.

Bending over excitedly, I smoothed it out on his knee and read the words written on it in ink. Apparently it was the beginning of a letter, which had been discontinued and thrown away. It read:

My Good Prince Rupert:

This is to say that your romantic career is at an end. Every dog, 'tis said, has his day, and yours — poor dog! — has come. You have been useful to me, I shall not deny, and I am grateful for a few things. For the rest — no matter! At any rate, I am through with you, and for good. It may be that your little enterprise —

* * *

There the fragment ended. I sat staring at it until Lavender snapped off his light and plunged us into darkness.

'Well?' he asked, and chuckled at my astonishment.

'That is a threatening letter, Lavender,' I said soberly. 'Did Lennard write it? There's no signature.'

'Oh, I have no doubt that he wrote it; Taggart could tell us. It was never finished, of course. He may have written another that pleased him more. A very curious letter! Did Parris receive one like it? Or was this written for us?'

'For us?'

'For any who would take the trail! It seems incredible that such a letter, preceding such a mystery, should have been left lying for anybody to find.'

'You can't ignore it, Jimmy,' I said.

'No, I can't! Furthermore, I must assume that its brother went to Parris, and that it had something to do with this double disappearance. On the face of it, it would appear that Lennard was threatening Parris, but the tone of the letter is not violent; it is more ironical than malicious. One might suppose such a line as 'your day has come,' to be a threat — or, such a line as 'I am through with you for good.' And yet the tone of the letter is rather one of amused pity, as if the writer had knowledge of the other's disgrace in some connection, and were twitting him about it.'

'I would arrest Lennard, just the same, on the strength of that letter,' I vigorously asserted.

'So would the police,' said Lavender. 'I'm not sure that I wouldn't arrest Parris on the strength of it!'

I stared at him for a moment, then nodded.

'I see your point, of course; but both are missing — Parris the more mysteriously of the two.'

He did not answer, and for a time there was silence between us while the auto scudded toward the Loop. Then Lavender broke the silence with another question.

'And why 'Prince Rupert'?'

'Part of Lennard's irony, no doubt,' I made answer. 'You pointed out the satirical tone of the letter.'

'Maybe,' he shrugged, 'but it has a romantic sound. That is, it suggests a masquerade. And Lennard obviously has something on Parris. May it not be that he has unmasked Parris, who is really somebody else? That would explain the letter in part. Parris's receipt of the letter — I wish it were dated! — would explain his rushing off to see Lennard and breaking his engagement for Sunday evening with Miss Valentine.'

I nodded agreement.

'Very ingenious, Jimmy,' I applauded, 'and it sounds more than plausible as you state it. I think it almost equally obvious, though, that Parris has something on Lennard.'

'Because Lennard, too, has disappeared? Perhaps! It's quite possible, of course. But if what Lennard knew about Parris was of great importance, as it seems to have been, Lennard may have disappeared for reasons best known to Parris.'

This gruesome suggestion gave me a shock.

'See how easily everything is explained by such a supposition,' he continued. 'Parris receives a letter and learns that he is discovered — whatever his sin may have been — so he hastens off to the *Beacon* office and sees Lennard. While there he calls Miss Valentine on the telephone, expecting that he will be through with Lennard in time to join her in an hour. Or did he really expect to meet her at all? The question intrudes itself! Assuming that he did, however, he is not through with Lennard in an hour, so we must believe that something unexpected happened. In other words, he was unable to shut up Lennard in one way, so he chose another. And it took him longer than an hour, and left him fearful of a return. Eh?'

I nodded again, unwillingly. I think I liked the unknown Parris better than Lavender did.

'Oh, I admit the plausibility of it,' I

said. 'Yet Lennard has found Parris 'useful,' by his own showing, and must have known of Parris's sin, whatever it was, for some time. Parris must have known that Lennard knew.'

'I think not,' disputed Lavender. 'Lennard undoubtedly had known Parris's secret for some time, but Parris may not have known that Lennard knew. When Lennard speaks of Parris as having been 'useful,' he means merely that he has used Parris for his own purposes — not that they were confidants.'

Beyond question, it occurred to me, Lavender already had constructed a strong theoretical case against Parris. I blurted out the plain American of his argument.

'It comes to this, then: That Parris has murdered Lennard to stop his mouth.'

'My dear Gilly, you know very well that I would never make such a charge with so little to go on. I do not even hint it, really, save as a possibility. I casually suggest it to you; I'm not telling the police. But you will admit, I think, that, if Lennard's body were to be found, some place, our task of locating Miss Valentine's fiancé would become a very unhappy one. In short, we should probably be looking for Lennard's murderer at the same time.'

★   ★   ★

At the Waterside Club we found Taggart impatiently awaiting us, although we were quite on time.

'We've only a moment for a bite, I'm afraid,' he greeted us. 'Lennard has been found, and — '

'Not in Milwaukee, surely?' interrupted Lavender, while something clutched at my heart.

'Milwaukee, hell!' said Taggart. 'He was found in the lake. Dead — drowned — probably a suicide. Poor old man!'

And there were tears in the eyes of Gorman B. Taggart.

3

It was true enough. Taggart identified the body while we looked on in silence. He had been telephoned at the club, and had only awaited our coming to hasten to the undertaking establishment whither his manager's body had been removed.

Lavender made his usual careful examination, but, startling as had been his suggestion in the taxicab, a suggestion that was almost prophecy, in one detail he had missed. To all appearances Lennard had not been murdered. The man had been drowned, but no mark showed on the body to indicate that violence had preceded the plunge. Lavender was frankly puzzled.

'Let's get out of here,' said Taggart suddenly! And when we were all back at the club he abruptly finished the thought that had been in his mind. 'Lavender, it's all my fault! I'm the man to blame! I threatened him with dismissal. Yes, I did!

After forty years of faithful service, I threatened him with dismissal! And why? Because the poor devil was drinking more than I thought he ought to. Poor old Lennard! And he went away and drowned himself! By God, I ought to be held responsible for it!'

Lavender shook his head in slow disagreement.

'No,' he said. 'Your feelings do you credit, of course, but you need not hold yourself responsible. You could not have anticipated this. I'm sorry that you didn't tell me sooner, though. Not that it would have made any difference to Lennard; he's been in the water since Sunday.'

'I'm to blame;' repeated Taggart grimly. 'A damned old fool, that's what I am! Well, the case is over, Lavender. I'm sorry. I hadn't looked for anything like this. I'll sign a check for whatever amount you like, and add a thousand to it for charity.'

This would not be at all to Lavender's liking, I thought, to give up the case. There was another side to it about which Taggart knew nothing. I looked anxiously at my friend, wondering what he would say. To my surprise he accepted his dismissal easily, accepting at the same time a handsome check for services, which, he declared, he had not rendered, and applauding Taggart's benevolent intentions toward 'charity.'

'There will be an inquest tomorrow,' he said, 'but I can't imagine that I shall be wanted. If so, you can communicate with me. And now, as I have another matter on hand, I'll thank you and say goodbye.'

We stood up and shook hands, and shortly thereafter were in the street, I wondering mightily. Lavender smiled at my perplexed face.

'I couldn't arouse his suspicions, Gilly,' he said. 'We must protect Miss Valentine's name at all costs. But, of course, I'm not through with the case. More than ever now, I must see it through. What, time is it? Late, of course! I wonder if that old chatterbox, Mrs. Barrett, is up at this hour? Probably not. I've got to see her again. She probably knows all about Lennard, and it's particularly necessary now for me to know all that she can tell.

Well, I'll have to wait until morning. And we shall have to see Miss Valentine again. What a muddle this Lennard episode has made of the case!'

But the morning brought our second and biggest shock; one that left us blinking. Miss Valentine called and calmly stopped the search. I had spent the night with Lavender, and we were hardly done with our breakfast when the young woman appeared.

'I've been thinking it over,' she told us, 'and I know now that I have acted foolishly. If Mr. Parris has seen fit to go away, it is his own business. It is mine, too, of course, but I have no right to make it anybody else's. If I have been — well, to be brutal, if I have been jilted, there is no reason for me to cry it from the housetops. And I am making myself ridiculous by seeking a man who may not care to have me find him. No, Mr. Lavender, let him come back to me, if there is a reasonable explanation for his action. I shall not demean myself by running after him.'

Lavender delicately pointed out that

her fiancé's disappearance had not been cried from the housetops, and was not likely to be; but his words fell on deaf ears. Nor did the suggestion that Parris might need our assistance move her to reconsider her decision.

There was no help for it. Lavender had been dismissed again, and when a few moments later she had gone away he said as much with bitter amusement. He had flatly declined to accept a fee from her, and I could see that he was greatly disturbed by this latest and apparently final development.

'I must admit that she did that very well,' he said with a snort. 'Now, why did she do it?'

'I thought she told us pretty clearly,' I replied. 'And, truth to tell, Lavender, there was sense in what she said — about running after him, you know.'

'That's the clever part of it,' he nodded. 'On the face of things, she has simply reconsidered and decided that she will not pursue a man who may not want her. But her agitation of yesterday does not check with her calmness of today.'

'Why else should she call us off?'

'Well,' drawled my friend, recovering his self-possession and lighting his pipe, 'it is just conceivable, you know, that she has heard from Parris!'

'By Jove!' I cried.

'That is too obvious not to be considered,' he continued; 'but there are difficulties in the way. If she has heard from Parris, and Parris is responsible for the death of Lennard, as he may very well be, then she is protecting him. She might even do that, of course, but somehow I don't think so. She doesn't really care enough about him for that. She may be protecting him without knowing the truth, or as I say, in spite of the truth. On the other hand, she may be perfectly honest in her statement to us. In any case, we seem to have been properly fired. How does it feel to be discharged, Gilly?'

'Are we definitely out of it?'

'Unless I carry my suspicions to the police, I fancy we are. And my suspicions are only suspicions. Lennard's body is unmarked. I could carry my tale to Taggart, perhaps, and work with him again; but that would be betraying Miss Valentine, which is not to be considered. It looks as if we were out of a job, Gilly!'

But we were not out long. Before our pipes had been refilled twice the telephone rang, and on the other end of the connection was Gorman B. Taggart. Taggart, too, had reconsidered.

'Look here, Lavender,' he said to my friend, as at Lavender's nod I picked up the extension receiver and listened in, 'has it occurred to you that there may have been something irregular in Lennard's death?'

'Yes,' replied Lavender promptly, 'it has! But there's not a shred of actual evidential proof. What makes you ask?'

'Nothing but my conscience, I'm afraid,' said Taggart mournfully. 'If I could think that I was not indirectly responsible for this, I'd be a happy man, Lavender.'

'Then,' said my friend, 'try to be happy. I can't promise anything, but if you want me to go ahead with my suspicions and see where they lead, I'll be glad to make the attempt.'

'Fine!' boomed the voice of Taggart. 'Go ahead! Unlimited funds behind you, and report when you've got something to report. Goodbye!'

Lavender hung up the receiver with a smile of wicked pleasure.

'We're never out of a job long, anyway,' he murmured. Then he bounded to his feet. 'Gilly, I'm off to see Lennard's housekeeper, the garrulous, and perhaps bibulous, Mrs. Barrett. You're off to see Miss Dale Valentine. Tell her of the finding of Lennard's body, if she doesn't know, and that Parris and Lennard are known to have been together. The Lennard affair is probably in the papers, and she may have seen it; possibly that's what brought her here this morning. Tell her, anyway, and try to find out whether she has heard directly or indirectly from Parris. Don't frighten her. We're asking for assistance, not threatening her; but she must understand that we are now employed by Taggart in this affair. You can explain that we have not betrayed her confidence. She'll see you, I think — I thought she liked your hair.'

101

He seized a handful of cigars and a package of cigarettes from his humidor, and we descended the stairs to the street, A gray-haired old man was approaching, our door, and at sight of us he stopped.

'Mr. Lavender?' he asked, glancing from one to the other of us. My friend nodded, and he continued: 'I am Arthur Valentine. My daughter, I believe, has consulted you about the curious absence of her fiancé, Mr. Rupert Parris. May I ask whether you have made any headway in the matter?'

Lavender seemed surprised. He shook his head.

'We are no longer in Miss Valentine's employ,' he said quietly. 'I believe Mr. Parris has not been found, but you will have to consult your daughter, Mr. Valentine.'

The old man, for whom a handsome car, was waiting, stared at us in astonishment.

'I'm afraid I don't understand you,' he said at length. 'My daughter said nothing to me about concluding the search. This is very strange. You know nothing, then?'

'Nothing whatever,' said Lavender politely. 'Have you any theory of your own?'

Valentine shook his head. 'I am not in my daughter's confidence in this matter,', he replied almost sadly. 'I was on my way to the office, and I thought I would stop in and see you. Until yesterday my daughter and I discussed this matter freely, but last night she seemed worried, and this morning she left the house early, refusing to talk. I thought that perhaps she had heard something that distressed her.'

'Not at all,' said Lavender cheerfully. 'Not from us, at any rate. She called this morning and dispensed with our services, Mr. Valentine; that is all I can tell you.'

With a word of thanks Valentine turned away. Lavender thoughtfully watched him until his machine had turned the corner and disappeared.

'Last night!' he said. 'What did Miss Valentine learn last night, Gilly, that made her refuse further to discuss matters with her father?'

After a moment he shrugged, and at

that instant a taxicab came into sight. He flagged it with upraised hand.

'A great day, eh?' he smiled, as if nothing had occurred to make him think. 'Better come back here, Gilly, when you're through. I'll return as quickly as possible.'

As luck would have it, Miss Valentine had not gone directly to her home, and in consequence she was not there when I called. I waited in the house for an hour, and spent another hour in the streets nearby; then as she had not appeared I returned to Lavender's rooms where he impatiently awaited me.

'Odd!' he commented, when he had heard what I had to tell. 'Well, we'll call her up from time to time. We must talk with her.'

'What about Mrs. Barrett?' I demanded.

'I begin to see light, Gilly,' he replied gravely. 'I fancy I know what Miss Valentine heard last night, or part of it; her father may have revealed something innocently enough which set her on the right track. I'll tell you the whole story, and you can see what you make of it.

This, in effect, is what Mrs. Barrett had to tell. She was prostrated, of course, by Lennard's death, and glad to tell everything she knew.

'Lennard came from Washburn, as she told us before. In his youth there was an unhappy love affair, as a result of which he never married. A Miss Mary Glover was his sweetheart, and on the eve of their wedding, almost, she jilted him and married a wealthy man in the city — that is, in Chicago. Prepare to be shocked. We met the wealthy man this morning.'

'Great Jupiter!' I cried. 'Not Valentine?'

'Jupiter and Jove, too,' he agreed. 'Yes, Arthur Valentine. In short, Lennard was engaged to marry Miss Valentine's mother, and was turned down cold for money. Who shall say what tortures he suffered and what revenges he planned? Lennard came to Chicago, and no doubt kept track of the social rise of the Valentines. He was fortunately situated in a newspaper office; he knew all that went on. In time Dale Valentine was born, and in time Mrs. Valentine died. Dale Valentine grew up into — well, you know into what she grew. She had suitors, among them Rupert Parris, who became the successful one.

'Here, then, would be a splendid opportunity for Lennard's deferred revenge. Jilted by the mother himself, if he could contrive to have the daughter jilted on her wedding eve how poetic would be his revenge! I don't defend this course; I say it may very well have occurred to him. Suppose then that he contrives to meet Parris, to do him services, and at the same time to learn something about Parris that is not to Parris's credit. We can learn nothing of Parris's past. It may have been anything. But would it be enough to threaten Parris with exposure? Would Parris vanish at a threat? Not necessarily. Lennard's hold would have to be pretty strong for that.

'But suppose Lennard combines with his threat of exposure some manufactured tale, say about Dale Valentine's mother, whose memory he both loves and loathes! If Parris were a gentleman he would resent it; if he were a coward in masquerade, probably he would not. But gentleman or coward, what would Parris do? I think he would try to stop Lennard's mouth, either for his own sake, or for the sake of Miss Valentine. Did he do it?'

'I'm afraid he did, Lavender,' I confessed. 'You make it seem very probable. But what hold could Lennard have had over Parris?'

'A queer one, you may be sure. It's almost the kernel of the riddle.'

'And what do you think Miss Valentine learned from her father?'

'Merely, perhaps that he had once had an unsuccessful rival in love whose name was Lennard. It would be enough. Miss Valentine would couple it with the story in the newspapers about the discovery of Lennard's body. Or perhaps she already knew, through her mother years ago, that Lennard had been her father's rival. If so, the newspaper story about Lennard would revive that memory. But I think something her father said put her on the track of the truth, for he told us that it was last night that she began to be preoccupied and silent. All of which, of course, would be insufficient to convince her of what is possibly the truth, if she had not heard from Parris. She must have received a letter last night, and I'd give a good deal to know what it revealed.'

I turned it all over in my head, and to me it seemed complicated enough to bother anybody. But one thing I was certain of.

'The time has come, Lavender, to tell Taggart the whole story,' I said flatly.

'Yes,' he agreed instantly, 'we must be frank with Taggart; we can't play two games now. He must print no word of the affair, of course; and I think he will not wish to, for it will reflect on Lennard to some extent — his own man.'

He swung to the telephone and called up the Valentine home.

'This is Gorman B. Taggart speaking,' he said deliberately into the mouthpiece, 'the publisher of the *Morning Beacon*. I wish to speak to Miss Valentine.' There was a silence and then his tone changed. 'Out?' he cried. 'Out of town? Are you sure? When did she leave? A letter, eh? I am very sorry; I have important news for her. Can you say where she went? To what station, then? A ten o'clock train! Yes, Mr. Taggart speaking! Now listen, please. I want you to remember what Miss Valentine wore to the train. It is important, for I am going to send a man to see her, and he must be able to identify her.'

After this there was a longer silence, at the end of which Lavender coolly said, 'Thank you,' and hung up. He was tremendously excited.

'Gone!' he cried. 'Gone out of town on a ten o'clock train, this morning. There was a letter last night, as I suspected. They deceived you at the house, Gilly. They knew then that she had gone.'

'Yes,' I said, 'gone to meet Parris!'

He swung back to the telephone and gave a strange number quickly. Then he asked an astonishing question.

'A young woman, dark and very pretty, wearing a heavy veil, was there this morning and asked to see the body of Moss Lennard. Was she allowed to see it?'

He listened to the reply, then with a

word of thanks rang off.

'Miss Valentine saw Lennard's body this morning, after leaving these rooms. She examined Lennard's garments. She went away in a taxicab. By George, Gilly, that girl has courage! It took nerve to do that!'

4

We found Taggart seated before a worn old desk in a private office on the glass door of which appeared the letters forming the name 'Moss Lennard,' and the words 'Circulation Manager.' The publisher swung about in his chair as we entered and seemed embarrassed at our coming. But he extended his big hand in welcome.

'Glad to see you,' he said. 'I've just been looking over poor old Lennard's desk.'

'Nothing wrong with his accounts, of course?' asked Lavender. 'I assumed that you had looked into them before.'

'Oh, that's all right. He was straight as a string. But I didn't know what the old desk would develop.'

'What have you found?'

'Nothing of interest, I guess; unless it's this! I didn't know Moss went in for light literature.'

He smiled and handed over a volume bound in green cloth, on the back of which appeared its flamboyant title, 'The Montreville Mystery.'

Lavender smiled. 'I know that yarn,' he said. 'It's a French detective story, translated into English. A good one, too. I haven't read it in years.' He laid it on his knee. A curious light danced in his eyes.

'Well, Lennard must have found it to his taste,' said Taggart. 'It appears to be well worn, although I haven't had time to look into it.'

'I'll take it along with me, if I may,' smiled Lavender boyishly. 'Do you mind? I'd like to read that yarn again. Also,' he added dryly. 'I'd like to see why it was of such interest to Moss Lennard.'

Taggart looked surprised, but readily acquiesced.

'Sure,' he said. 'I guess no one wants it now. Keep it if you care to.'

'Now,' said my friend when he had pocketed the volume, 'I have news for you, Mr. Taggart, and you are going to be surprised.' And he told our client the whole story of Rupert Parris.

Taggart was immensely agitated. He leaped from his chair and executed a few steps of an improvised and unintentional dance.

'We've got to get him!' he cried. 'Lavender, we've got to get him!'

'I suppose so,' said Lavender. 'But wait; I'm not through.' And he revealed the recent activities of Miss Dale Valentine, including a statement of her visit to the morgue where the body of Lennard lay.

Taggart paced the room in his excitement.

'You see it, of course he demanded. 'Incriminating evidence! She removed something from the garments that would have hurt Parris!'

'And now she's gone to Parris,' I said, unintentionally humorous.

'No,' corrected Lavender, 'she's gone to Washburn, Illinois, the early home of Moss Lennard and her mother. She must have relatives there yet. The poor child has discovered the truth.'

'The truth!' cried Taggart suspiciously. 'What are you withholding now, Lavender. Come, let's have it! What is the truth then?'

'It's a long story,' my friend replied, 'and I've just found the final link in this novel you have given me. But the first truth is this: Moss Lennard was not murdered; he committed suicide, and for the purpose of making it appear that Parris had murdered him. He wished to leave a stigma upon the name of Rupert Parris, the accepted lover of Miss Dale Valentine. It was part of his revenge upon the girl's mother, long dead. You know that story. With the girl jilted and her lover's name smirched, his revenge would be complete save in one particular.

'He would want Miss Valentine to know what he had done; that would be the final twist of the knife, to tell her what he had done and why he had done it. I am now convinced that the letter Miss Valentine received was from Lennard, a letter nicely timed to be delivered some days after his death. It would be sent first to some other part of the country, then re-addressed by some friend there, who, of course, would not suspect Lennard's motive. Miss Valentine received it last night, probably by special delivery.' I can see Lennard

114

working it all out.

'What a dolt I have been, Gilly!' he exclaimed. 'Because the truth was fantastic I refused to see it, or at any rate to credit it, until this book and the girl herself convinced me. She left the house veiled. Why? I deduced the morgue, and found that I was right. I had already deduced a letter, and I know now that I was right. Then Taggart hands me this book, and it is a book that I know! In it there is a leading character named Rupert; the scene of the story is Paris. Could anything be plainer? Look!'

He drew it from his pocket and began to turn the leaves. A quick frown settled between his eyes. Then suddenly he examined the covers. In the end he leaned back and laughed quietly.

'I've been an ass again,' he smiled. 'An examination of the book would have solved the mystery days ago, had we known of the book's existence. Look at it! A book on theatrical make-up, rebound in the covers of a popular novel!'

But now Taggart and I were both on our feet, bursting with the amazing thought that had pierced our brains.

'Then Parris — ' I began, and hesitated to finish it.

'Was Lennard!' roared Taggart.

'Yes,' smiled Lavender. 'Lennard, all the time, except for one or two evenings a week, when he became Parris to avenge himself upon the daughter of the woman who had jilted him. Gilly, I'm afraid I am becoming dull!'

5

We did not pursue the distressed and humiliated girl to Washburn. Lavender's explanation was too clear to require further proof. Complete and final proof was found by a thorough ransacking of Lennard's rooms in the West Side rooming house, where the paraphernalia of make-up, and a really splendid toupee, was carefully hidden away. But the make-up boxes were scarcely touched; they had been unnecessary except at the beginning.

Mrs. Barrett, half blind and splendidly loyal to her eccentric guest, had never suspected, and in the dark hallway — on the evenings of his Parris masquerades, as Lavender called them — Lennard had passed without question. Dressed in Lennard's clothes and speaking in Lennard's voice, he had gone forth as Parris to exchange for Parris's clothes at his hotel. His 'Parris' life had been spent in

117

three places, almost alternately; at his hotel, at his club, and at the Valentine home, and at no one of them had he ever stayed long. It was a masterpiece of deception.

His motive for suicide was certainly obscure; but it is conceivable that he may, have sickened of the game he was playing. Lavender's idea is that he was merely sick of life, and passed out gladly after accomplishing his self-appointed task. Certainly the whole scheme was elaborately worked out, even to the ingeniously phrased and romantic letter in which the manager bade farewell to his younger self, then left for an investigator to find. And an admirable touch was his habit of calling himself from the hotel — that is, calling for Lennard on the telephone, in the hearing of the operator who knew him as Parris. A clever rascal on the whole, and a man who might have been an asset to society with a little more charity.

'The amazing thing to me, Lavender,' I said, 'is how he was able to pass himself off in the Valentine home.'

'It may have been difficult at first,' he

replied, 'but Lennard's make-up was, of course, very skilful. It consisted in very little, for really little disguise was necessary. He probably used very little theatrical make-up, in spite of his study of the subject. Lennard was fifty and more, but a well-preserved man. Further, he was thin, and therefore had no betraying weight to endanger his plan; he would pass as a slim, middle-aged man. With a good wig over his half-bald head, and a sprinkling of rice powder over a good massage, he would look quite as young as he claimed to be. He admitted to forty-one years! His dress helped, too, for naturally he dressed in the height of fashion. His features were good, and his determination was great.

'And the big thing in his favor was the fact — for certainly it must have been a fact — that neither Mr. Valentine nor his daughter ever had seen him as Lennard. The mother who would have recognized him was dead. Probably he met the girl's father at the club and won him by his personality and his chess; after that the match was as good as made. Miss

Valentine as much as hinted that it was a match made by her father.'

'I am sorry for Dale Valentine,' I said sincerely.

'So am I,' said Lavender, 'sorry that she must suffer this humiliation, even though there may be no distressing publicity, for Taggart will take care of that. Parris will be called away suddenly, and will die in another city, and no one will know the difference. But I'm glad for Dale Valentine in another sense. What a good thing it is that the old rascal didn't see the greater revenge he had in his power. Suppose he had actually married the girl!'

The Dorrington
Diamonds

1

'And when I turned around the diamonds were gone!'

Mrs. Baker's voice cracked on a high note of anguish. I stepped forward hastily.

'There, there!' I said, patting her shoulder. Somewhere I had read that this was the way to quiet an agitated woman; at least, it is the way it is always done in fiction.

Listening to my landlady's story, my mind at once had leaped to my friend Lavender, that successful dilettante detective, and I was upon the point of mentioning him to Mrs. Baker; but my soothing hand failed in its magic. She shook herself out of my grasp as if she were twenty instead of fifty, and I an impudent admirer.

'Don't be foolish, Mr. Gilruth!' she snapped. 'It's not petting and comforting I want. It's help. Please understand. You *do* understand, don't you, that they were not my diamonds? But I'm responsible for what goes into that safe; and I tell you honestly I don't think the whole place would sell for enough to make it up to Mr. Dorrington. Oh, what shall I do? Tell me what to *do!*'

She turned on me so fiercely that for a moment I wondered if she suspected me of the theft. Back of her furious distraction, however, lay tears and a complete breakdown; I was a good enough medical student (although only in my second year) to see that. She had complimented me by asking my assistance.

Well, I was flattered; and like the idiot that I was I determined to say nothing about Lavender. I would solve this mystery myself! When the case was successfully concluded — I liked that word case — I would tell Lavender about it, and receive his felicitations. Certainly I knew enough about Lavender's methods by this time. So my thoughts ran.

'You haven't told Mr. Dorrington yet?' I asked, in my best professional manner.

Mrs. Baker, withholding her tears, gave

me a glance of the deepest scorn.

'Mr. Dorrington left the city last night, as I told you,' she answered. 'How could I have told him?'

'Of course,' I said hastily. 'What I intended to ask is whether you have said anything to your husband?'

A frightened look crossed her face. She shook her head.

'No,' she whispered. 'I — I can't tell him — yet. He would — oh, you know what he would say!'

I knew; and I almost stroked her shoulder again. Baker, the husband of my landlady, was an abominable individual. He posed as something of an invalid, lived on his wife's earnings, and was supposed to be unable to do any but the lightest labor. His fragility, however, seemed equal to the strain of riding into the Loop district several times a week to meet a number of cronies, and to the almost constant association of a blackened pipe, in which he smoked the most atrocious tobacco I had ever inhaled as vapor. On top of this, he was a querulous, sarcastic beast, whom on general principles I longed to kick. I knew what he would say to the revelation of the missing diamonds. Without seeming to blame his wife, he would make her life miserable with his covert, sneering comment: and further, he would pity himself to the point of my complete exasperation.

'Look here, Mrs. Baker,' I said. 'Let's have a look at the safe, you and I. Quietly! We won't say anything about this affair to anyone else for a while. How long will Mr. Dorrington be away?'

'Two weeks,' she said hopelessly.

'Good,' I cried. 'That will give us plenty of time to work. You don't suspect anybody?'

'I don't know what to think. I'm at my wits' end, Mr. Gilruth. I spoke to you because I didn't know which way to turn.'

I visibly swelled. Why am I always an ass?

'Could it have been burglars?'

'Who else could it have been?' she asked simply. 'And yet, there are no marks on the safe,' she wearily added.

'Ah, the safe!' I said. 'Let us have a look at it, now.'

As for the burglar theory, I had my own

doubts. It seemed to me an inside job. The diamonds, I thought, could not be of any great value. I had seen them, as a matter of fact; at least, I had seen Dorrington with certain unset stones. He was a dealer, and no doubt they were good enough stones; but I doubted that their value would be more than one thousand dollars, all told. Mrs. Baker's notion that they represented a fortune seemed silly. But I did not tell her any of my thoughts. She was right about the safe, though. There was not a mark on it to suggest tampering. We paused before it, looking accusingly at the black metal box. I tried the handle, but of course the door was locked. It was a small safe and opened with a key.

'I locked it after discovering the theft,' murmured my landlady, with a wan smile. She looked around cautiously to be sure we were not overheard.

'May I see the key?'

But the key had no marks, which, to my eye, seemed suspicious. I could imagine Lavender looking at it through his pocket glass, but I carried no such tool. I looked unutterably wise as I handed back the key and asked her to open the safe. 'It was on this little shelf here — the package was,' she said, pointing out the spot where it had lain.

Greatly excited, I leaned over to look. Sure enough, there had been a small package in the place indicated. Though an excellent housekeeper, Mrs. Baker apparently did not bother to dust the shelves of her safe. And certainly where once the package had reposed there was now no package. This proved — What did it prove? It dawned on me that it proved only what we already knew — that the package of diamonds was missing. It proved only that Mrs. Baker was telling the truth, which I never had doubted.

I began to think again of Lavender. This amateur detective business, while fascinating, was less simple than it appeared to one merely looking on while another — and he an expert — did the thinking.

An idea struck me, rather sharply.

'Look here,' I said. 'You're sure you didn't give them back to Mr. Dorrington?'

Her glance spoke volumes of contempt. 'You might have, you know, and have forgotten,' I added with dignity.

'Do you think we ought to send for the police?' she asked.

'If you please,' I coldly replied.

'Oh, Mr. Gilruth,' she cried, 'don't think I don't appreciate your kindness, but this doesn't seem to be a case for you and me. I've got to get those diamonds before Mr. Dorrington gets back, or I'm ruined. Don't you see? I've got to have help, Mr. Gilruth!' The tears now were standing in her eyes. In a moment she would be sobbing. My insane egotism suddenly left me.

'By George, you shall have help,' I violently promised. 'The best help in America! Cheer up, Mrs. Baker. I'm off to telephone — and not to the police.'

She stared after me as if I were quite mad. But this time I knew exactly what I was doing.

I gave the operator the number of my friend, James Eliot Lavender, A. M., and Jimmy Lavender was at home.

2

He had a way with women. I may have said this before, in speaking of my friend Lavender; but it is only the truth. Ten minutes after his prompt arrival, Lavender metaphorically owned the rooming house, and so far as Mrs. Baker was concerned the mystery was as good as solved. She saw her diamonds — Dorrington's diamonds, rather — returned by nightfall, without scandal, and the immediate resumption of life's normal round. She shifted her burden to the shoulders of my friend with grateful trust and prompt relief. Her immediate and complete confidence in my likeable companion touched Lavender. I noted with amazement that with his hand upon her shoulder, Mrs. Baker made no effort to shake herself free. Yet she had known this man for ten minutes, while me she had known for three years.

At the door, I had given Lavender a

brief account of the loss and the circumstances leading up to it, as I knew them; but he insisted on hearing the story again from Mrs. Baker's lips.

He listened patiently to her rather disjointed narrative, asking occasional questions to help her along.

'That is very clear indeed,' said Lavender, when she had finished. 'Mr. Gilruth tells me that he rather shocked you by inquiring whether you might have returned the package to Mr. Dorrington; but at least it is the first question.'

'I certainly did not return it to Mr. Dorrington,' was the prompt and decisive reply.

'That is settled, then,' smiled my friend. 'When did you first discover the loss, Mrs. Baker? I mean, at exactly what hour?'

'It was just a little after seven o'clock this morning. I always open the safe the first thing in the morning, to be sure everything is all right. I've never lost anything before!'

With the last line there were symptoms of tears, as she thought again of the bare shelf the early sunlight had shown her.

'It was a very small package, was it not? Yes, I should have thought so. And, of course, you have been all through the safe, to be quite sure it has not been mislaid among the other things?'

Mrs. Baker had been through everything. To my surprise Lavender did not himself repeat the search, but accepted her statement.

'What does your husband think of it?' asked my friend suddenly.

I had forgotten to mention Baker in my narration, and now I regretted the omission. Mrs. Baker colored.

'He doesn't know about it yet.' she answered, in a low voice, and I contrived gently to kick Lavender's ankle. She added, a bit indignantly, 'Mr. Baker, so far as I know, did not know that the package existed!'

'Quite so,' agreed the unperturbed Lavender. 'Well, let us have a little rehearsal of what happened last night. What exactly were you doing, Mrs. Baker, when Mr. Dorrington gave you the diamonds?'

'I was sitting right here at this table. I was going to send some money to the bank, and I was writing out the slip — '

'I see. And, of course, you did send the money? Good! Now by whom did you send your money to the bank, Mrs. Baker?'

'By — but it is not the money I have lost, Mr. Lavender. I wish it were.'

'That is true, but I am just establishing the whole scene of last night. It may help you to recall other details.'

'I sent the money by my servant, Maud Image,' said my landlady. 'It was not very much — only forty dollars.'

'And no doubt Maude Image is a thoroughly trusted person. Naturally, or you would not have sent her with money.'

'She has been with me for years,' said Mrs. Baker. 'She has taken money to the bank oftener than I've taken it myself, I guess. Mr. Gilruth can tell you about — '

'Yes,' I interrupted, somewhat importantly. 'Mrs. Baker is right about Maude Image, Lavender.'

'I don't doubt it for a moment,' my friend, with a wicked smile at me. 'May I see your bank-book, Mrs. Baker?'

That, too, was in the safe, and in a moment he was examining it.

'Quite correct,' observed Lavender easily. 'Forty dollars received, and the deposit neatly initialed by the clerk who received it. So Maude Image delivered the money and then returned. I suppose she returned, eh?'

'Oh, yes! She's in the kitchen, sir, now.'

'A curious place for an image,' smiled Lavender, 'but we shall leave her there for the present. So here you were, filling out the deposit slip for the Image, when in came Mr. Dorrington with his diamonds. You knew they were diamonds, didn't you?'

'Yes, of course. He told me.'

'Excellent! And he asked you to take care of them for him until he came back. And you — what did you do, exactly?'

'I went right on filling out my slip. I was very busy, you see, and I wanted to get Maude off to the bank. And while I was writing, Mr. Dorrington was talking. He asked if he could put the package in the safe, and I said, 'Yes, of course,' and so he did — '

'The dickens he did!' said Lavender. 'You mean that he, himself, placed the package in the safe?'

'Yes, sir, with his own hands.'

'The safe was open?'

'Yes, sir. I was getting the money out, you see, and my bank-book.'

'I see. So he put his package in, on this shelf, while you were writing out your slip. Did you see the package after he had put it on the shelf?'

'Of course, I did. I particularly looked around when he asked me to, and watched him put it on the shelf.'

'He asked you to watch him?'

'He did, Mr. Lavender. He said, 'You see, Mrs. Baker, where I'm putting it?' And I looked at it there in its place.'

'Then what happened?'

'Then he talked for a little while about his trip, and went away.'

'Only about his trip?'

'I believe that is all, Mr. Lavender.'

Lavender looked at me as if he were bewildered. I wondered if he, too, had reached the end of his rope, he looked so stumped. I feebly smiled. Then he smiled, and I thought his grin was almost diabolic.

'How long after Mr. Dorrington left did you lock up the safe?' he began again, turning to my landlady. 'Was it at once?'

'Y-yes,' she replied, with the first hesitation I had noticed. 'It was very soon after he went away, anyway. But Maude had just come in, and I gave her the money and sent her to the bank. I locked the safe right after she left. There wasn't any more than a minute or two between the time Mr. Dorrington left and the time I locked the safe. And I was right here at this table all that time.'

Lavender scratched his head, and again I thought him at sea. His glance as it rested on mine seemed troubled. And then his left eyelid quivered slightly, as if he would have liked to have winked. Apparently, then, he was highly amused. What he could find in the situation to laugh at, I could not imagine; but then, Lavender's humor was always beyond me.

'You are quite certain you did not lock

the safe until after the Image had gone?' he asked.

This reiterated reference to her servant as 'the Image,' had its effect. Mrs. Baker smiled, slowly at first, then more swiftly and widely. Lavender chuckled.

'Quite sure,' answered my landlady. 'When she came in, I remember, I had just finished writing out the slip, and I put it in the bag with the money — you know the little paper bags the bank gives you for money. I sent her away. Then I turned around and closed and locked the safe.'

'Good!' said Lavender, briskly. 'That is all very well remembered, Mrs. Baker. Now for the one important question! When you shut the safe are you sure the package of diamonds was there?'

Mrs. Baker stared incredulously.

'Why, of course!' she said at length. 'I saw him put it there!'

'You saw Mr. Dorrington put it there; but after he had gone, and before you locked the safe, did you see it again?'

'Why,' cried Mrs. Baker, 'I — I must — '

'You must have seen it? Because you saw him put it there, eh? No, that doesn't follow, Mrs. Baker. Look here.' And my friend laughed outright. 'I'll bet the package was not there when you closed and locked the safe!'

'Where was it?' I asked. Mrs. Baker was beyond speech.

'In Mr. Dorrington's pocket.'

'No!' my landlady cried shrilly. I weakly echoed her denial.

'Yes!' said Lavender, with his cheerful boyish grin. 'I'll prove it to you both before evening, if you have Dorrington's address. It is very simple. You admit that you were busy, and I think you are not too certain about what Mr. Dorrington said to you. When — '

'You think Dorrington stole his own diamonds?' I interrupted.

'He changed his mind,' said Lavender. 'When he decided not to leave the package, Mrs. Baker did not hear his remark, and later she closed the safe convinced that the package was there — solely because she had seen him put it there, and had not seen him remove it.'

Mrs. Baker grasped at the straw.

'Oh, if I could believe that! It might — it might be — '

'Of course, it might,' smiled Lavender. 'Indeed, it is. Come now, tell me Mr. Dorrington's address, and I'll send him a wire this afternoon. His response will settle the whole thing; then if I'm wrong, I'll admit it.'

He chuckled again.

'He is in Aurora,' said Mrs. Baker. 'At the Liberty Hotel. That is the address he left with me; but I think he was going farther. He may be gone. Oh, if you can only reach him!'

'And if you are only right!' I added.

'What a cheerful person you are, Gilly!' grinned Lavender. 'What do you want me to do? Make a cash wager?'

I shook my head.

'No,' I said; 'I know you too well, Jimmy. If you say it's so, I must believe you; but surely Mrs. Baker can believe her own eyes. And Dorrington wouldn't be as casual about it as you make out.'

My friend shrugged.

'Oh man of little faith!' he said, cryptically.

'You have relieved my mind more than I can tell you,' burst out Mrs. Baker suddenly. 'Oh, Mr. Lavender, don't disappoint me!'

Lavender laid his hand on her shoulder again, and smiled into her eyes. And my middle-aged landlady almost purred! In a moment, however, she was embarrassed, for the door opened and a woman entered.

The newcomer was older than Mrs. Baker, and was known to me as Maude Image, a fact I attempted to communicate to Lavender. But he had placed her at once. He took her in with a swift glance, from her gray hair and powerful spectacles to her gnarled old hands and her slowly-moving feet.

'Pardon, ma'am,' she nodded, as she came forward, 'but am I to go to the bank today?'

Something happened in Lavender's brain. I can always tell when he is seized of a new thought. Before my landlady could reply, my friend's chain-lightning mind had functioned.

'Mr. Gilruth will be passing the bank

shortly,' he swiftly observed. 'We shall be walking that way.'

'Yes,' I said, stupidly.

Mrs. Baker seemed puzzled.

'Very well,' she said, at length. 'Thank you. Then you needn't mind, Maude. Mr. Gilruth will carry the money.'

The elderly servitor nodded shortly and withdrew, followed by the eyes of my friend Lavender.

'Hardly a safe messenger, I should say,' he commented as the door closed behind her. 'Did you notice her spectacles, Gilly? She must be nearly blind as a bat. Well, shall we be getting along?'

I went for my hat, while Mrs. Baker made ready her small bag of notes and silver. It was Saturday, and the bank closed early, so that we were starting some hours before Maude's regular time. When I returned, Lavender was smoking a cigarette on the doorstep, and my landlady was looking at him as a mother looks at a well-loved son. She handed me the little bag without a word, and with a lift of our hats we went down the steps.

'I'm a thousand times obliged to you,

Lavender,' I said, as we walked the avenue.

'Not at all,' he replied. 'it's really an interesting exercise; and in return for your numerous services to me I am very happy to relieve your friend's anxiety.'

I laughed. My numerous services to my friend had consisted largely in watching his movements with ever-increasing admiration, while contriving to get in his way on every conceivable occasion.

'You really think Dorrington has the diamonds?' I asked after a moment.

'You shall see his telegram,' said Lavender, 'inside of two hours. I'm off now to send mine. After you've delivered your consignment of currency, you might follow me to my rooms.'

He turned the next corner and left me, with a final, whimsical, appraising smile. His smiles always bothered me with a sense of my own stupidity. As I entered the door of Mrs. Baker's bank it occurred to me to wonder why my friend had wished me to act as messenger instead of Maude Image; but he was beyond questioning.

In the bank I received some information that sent me questing back, mentally, to my earlier thoughts. We had almost forgotten Henry Baker, my landlady's disagreeable husband. He was recalled to my mind by the accident of my being a stranger at the bank.

The young man who received the deposit looked keenly at me, recognizing a stranger.

'Anything wrong with the old lady who usually comes?' he asked courteously.

'No,' I said. 'I room with Mrs. Baker, and happened to be coming this way. That's all.'

'I see,' he smiled. 'All well at the Elms?'

The Elms was the extravagant name of my rooming house.

'Quite well,' I answered, in some surprise.

'Mr. Baker still complaining?'

'About as usual,' I replied, and had to smile, although my surprise was increasing. 'You know him?'

'Yes,' he said frankly. 'He used to bring the money here; but I hadn't seen him for some time, until the other day, I met him

143

in the street.' Lowering his voice, he confidently added, 'I suppose you know he lost a bit of money on the market lately?'

'Really,' I returned, 'I'm not in Mr. Baker's confidence.'

'All right,' he laughed. 'Then you needn't say I told you.'

Very much puzzled, I left the bank. Suddenly I was furiously angry with Baker. The bank clerk's remark had opened my eyes. Baker was dabbling with the market; and in some cheap bucket shop or other. This was what happened to his wife's earnings. This was why, in spite of an apparently prosperous rooming house, the total of the figures in her bankbook was so small. I longed to seek out Henry Baker and thrash him, invalid or no.

Another idea occurred to me. Could it be possible that the bank clerk knew something more about Baker? Was the young fellow trying to tell me something he thought I ought to know? Was Lavender wrong about Dorrington? In short, was Baker the thief, as I had at first suspected? Baker had lost money on the market. I had only the clerk's word for it, to be sure; but the truth easily could be established.

With long steps I set out for Lavender's rooms, and arrived to find that my friend had not yet put in an appearance. In a state of mingled anger and excitement, induced by my thoughts of Baker, I smoked on the Lavender doorstep and watched the comings and goings of trains in the elevated station across the way. I waited exactly an hour, at the end of which time I had settled the mystery in my own mind. When would Lavender come?

He materialized at my side, the same quizzical smile in place. Into his astonished ears I poured the story I had heard and the story I had deduced. When I had finished, he handed me a telegram.

'I waited for it at the office,' he said, 'and was fortunate in catching Dorrington at his hotel.'

The telegram said briefly:

Package safe in my hands home tonight explain in person.

3

I saw Dorrington the next morning, and he confirmed his telegram. The day was Sunday, and he was smoking and reading the Sunday newspaper in Mrs. Baker's amazing plush parlor. He had seen Lavender the night before, having gone directly to my friend's rooms upon his arrival in Chicago.

Mrs. Baker, of course, was in ecstasies. 'Poor soul!' said Dorrington. 'She must have been frightened half to death. And I'm afraid I gave her an after-shock, this morning, when I told her the value of the stones. She had supposed them worth about $5,000 — a fortune to her, of course — but $25,000 would be closer to the truth. It was the value of the stones that made me hesitate at the last minute about leaving them with her, although her strong box seemed safe enough, and certainly was the last place a thief would look for a package of valuable diamonds.

But I hesitated and decided against it.'

'What did you say to her?' I curiously asked.

'You mean the night I left? Friday? I said to her, 'On second thought, Mrs. Baker, I think I shall take the diamonds with me. That will relieve you of worry.' And she replied, 'Yes!' Just 'Yes,' mind you. Of course, I thought she had heard and understood; but apparently her mind was on something else.'

'Well,' I said, 'I'm glad it has turned out as well as it has, and sorry you had to be brought home.'

'Oh,' he replied, 'I had to come, anyway, or I should not have bothered after your friend's telegram and my response. I've delayed my main trip for a few weeks. A wonderful fellow!'

'Who? Lavender? Yes!' I cried heartily. 'If you ever do lose any diamonds, you'll know whom to look up.'

'I shall indeed.'

The 'wonderful fellow' himself, however, I did not see for two weeks. I was busy with an examination at the college, and he was busy on the single evening upon which I had found opportunity to call him on the telephone; so our ways had lain apart, as I say, for a fortnight. At the end of this interval, I was flattered to receive a telephone call from him. It was usually the other way round, and I was pleased by this mark of attention.

I was to meet him at his rooms at eight o'clock, that evening; that was all. He abruptly rang off, and I decided that he was very busy indeed.

Eight o'clock, however, found me ready to hand, for at that hour to the minute I pushed his doorbell.

Lavender had another visitor when I entered the room, and to my intense astonishment, when the man rose to greet me, I saw that it was Dorrington. He smiled broadly at my bewilderment, which was explicable by the fact that I had seen him at the rooming house not an hour before, at which time he had said nothing about expecting to call on Lavender.

I shook hands with him as if we were meeting for the first time, and then I laughed.

'Let me guess,' I said. 'You have lost your diamonds again, and have followed my advice and come to Lavender! How's that?'

'Not bad,' said Dorrington. 'It's very near to the truth, at any rate. My diamonds certainly have disappeared, and I'm hoping that Mr. Lavender may help me to recover them. Shall I tell him?' he asked, looking at Lavender.

'Oh, yes,' smiled my friend. 'He is reasonably safe.'

Dorrington chuckled, as if he had a great joke to spring.

'Who do you suppose offered to sell me some diamonds, this evening, Mr. Gilruth?' he inquired, much in the manner of a minstrel show interlocutor.

Not knowing the answer to this riddle, I said — ungrammatically — 'Whom?'

'Who, Gilly!' reproved Lavender.

'Henry Baker!' said Dorrington.

'The devil!' I cried.

'Hardly that,' remarked Lavender. 'Baker is fairly harmless, although very much of a cad, and certainly something of an ass.'

'Tell me,' I ordered impatiently.

'Well,' continued Dorrington, 'it was just before dinner, and he came to me rather secretly asking, 'I say, Dorrington, you buy diamonds, don't you?' A bit off-hand, you know, as if it were unimportant, but still he would like to know. As everybody who knows me at all knows that I buy diamonds, I thought his question just a trifle superfluous. I told him that I did, and he opened up in a more confidential manner. It seemed that a friend of his was rather hard up, and wanted to sell his mother's jewels — among them a necklace which had been broken up in order to dispose of the stones separately.

'He dug into his pocket and produced a leather bag from which he rolled into my astonished palm my own diamonds!'

Lavender exploded at the look I turned upon him.

'The old scoundrel!' I said, at length. 'What did you do? Kept them, of course!'

'No,' said Dorrington sadly. 'I was tempted to keep them, I'll admit, and to tell him a great many things that I had been saving up. Fortunately, I had been coached by your friend, Mr. Lavender, for just such an emergency. I told Baker politely but firmly that I did not do business out of hours, and that he must come to my office tomorrow, and bring his friend with him. He protested that his friend couldn't come, which makes me strongly suspect that there is no friend; but when he found I was adamant, he promised to appear with the owner of the diamonds.'

This narrative agitated my thinking apparatus strangely.

'Great Scott!' I burst forth. 'But he knows they're your diamonds, Dorrington. He must. He stole them. He'll never show up tomorrow. I don't know what madness possessed him even to show them to you. He must be crazy!'

'To the contrary,' observed Lavender easily, 'he doesn't know they're Dorrington's diamonds. How should he? His wife told him nothing about the affair of the safe. It was her first thought, you remember, to keep it from him. Wherever he got them, he doesn't know they are Dorrington's; that is certainly suggested by his bringing them to Dorrington.'

'You think he has an accomplice?'

'I don't,' said Dorrington. 'Mr. Lavender thinks he may have.'

'He'll have to have one tomorrow,' said Lavender, 'since he's promised to bring this fake friend of his.'

'But where did he get them?' I asked vociferously. 'Did you put them in the safe again?'

'They haven't been placed in the safe, since the night I put them there under Mrs. Baker's eyes,' smiled Lavender.

There were two meanings to that. I gasped.

'You mean that — that they were stolen then, and never have been recovered?'

'Just that,' said my friend. Dorrington nodded.

'But you said — ' I looked at the diamond man, then back at Lavender. At this point, the modicum of brain that I boast performed its duty.

'The telegram was a fake then,' I cried; 'and Dorrington didn't have the package, after all!'

'Excellent, Gilly!' grinned Lavender.

'Now we are getting on. It's a shame to tease, you, old man,' he swiftly added. 'You are quite right. I got Dorrington on the long distance wire, that afternoon, told him what had happened, asked him to keep quiet and let on he had the diamonds, and then faked that telegram myself.'

'Why?' I asked.

'Why!' said my friend impatiently. 'Well, for two reasons. First, to quiet the mind of your good Mrs. Baker; second, to allay the suspicions of the person who removed the diamonds. We wanted him (or her) to think that he (or she) had succeeded in his (or her) attempt at crime. Comprenny? He (or she) would then make some effort to dispose of the diamonds, and would be apprehended in that effort. *Quod erat demonstrandum.*'

I smiled.

'And he has now done so, eh?'

'To wax sensational,' said Lavender, 'we are certainly 'hot on the trail'.'

'And what happens tomorrow?'

'Tomorrow the shrewd Henry Baker comes to the office of our friend

153

Dorrington and repeats his offer to sell the diamonds. I shall be there, and you shall be there, to endeavor to make clear to him the error of his ways.'

Another thought paralyzed my brain.

'Look here, Lavender,' I said. 'You keep saying 'him or her.' You think that a woman may have done this?'

He looked me in the eyes, smiling.

'If you have any women friends whom you are inclined to suspect,' he replied, 'I shall ask you, in the interests of justice, not to warn them, Gilly.'

Dorrington laughed outright and picked up his hat.

'Come along, Mr. Gilruth,' he said. 'We can't do anything with this fellow in his present mood. He's having a good time at our expense. Good night, Mr. Sherlock Holmes!'

Lavender's chuckle floated down the stairs after us.

'Now,' said Dorrington, when we were in the street, 'about tomorrow. You are up rather early, I think? Perhaps it would be better if you were to leave the house before I do, and wait for me at my Office.

It might not do for us to be seen leaving the house together. Baker might smell a rat, eh?'

'He might,' I said cynically.

'Oh, Baker's not altogether a fool. Never underestimate your opponent, you know!'

'Well, I'll be on hand when you arrive,' I promised.

'Good! And Lavender won't be long after you, I fancy!'

In point of fact, Lavender was there before either of us. I found him when I arrived, loitering in the lobby of the building in which Dorrington maintained an office.

'The appointment is for nine o'clock,' he remarked, as I joined him. 'Baker's appointment. We're cutting it rather fine, I think. Ah, here's Dorrington now, getting out of a taxi. Good morning! I think we had better go up at once.'

Dorrington thought so, too, and we entered an elevator together, when we were quite sure there was no Baker in sight.

It was a snug little office into which we

were ushered by its tenant, but we had little time in which to admire it. With Lavender, I went at once into a small inner chamber, where we were to wait while Dorrington received his visitors.

'I'm afraid of only one thing,' said Lavender in a low voice. 'That is, that Baker will come alone.'

'You don't believe him alone in the theft?'

'I don't think he had anything to do with it!' was my friend's surprising response. I looked at him in amazement.

'Then,' I suddenly accused, 'you think Mrs. Baker, herself — '

'No,' said Lavender, with a smile. 'I was only teasing you. I knew you were thinking of Mrs. Baker, and it pleased me to worry you for a moment.'

He stood up quickly.

'A close call,' he, whispered. 'Here they are — ahead of time! If they had seen you, downstairs, there might have been an escape. Fortunately, they don't know me. Quiet, now!'

A door beyond ours had opened and closed. Then a small window, closed with a sliding shutter, suddenly was opened in our wall; through it, although unseen ourselves, we could glimpse the top of Dorrington's head as he sat at his desk with his back to us. The voices in the outer room came clearly to our ears.

'Good morning!' boomed that of Dorrington. 'Mr. Baker, how are you? If I was short with you yesterday you will forgive me. I hope? I particularly dislike doing business in my hours of recreation.'

'*Huh!*' whispered Lavender admiringly.

'You have the diamonds with you? Yes, of course; and this is the friend who wishes to dispose of them? Very good!'

'My friend has a cold,' came the voice of Baker, 'so you will excuse — '

Dorrington chuckled expansively.

'Now that we have the diamonds,' he said, 'we shall excuse anything. You will not mind my showing them to my associate, who is in the inner office? Just a moment.'

His raised voice, in this connection, was our signal to enter. At the last word, Lavender opened the door and we stepped through and into the room.

'Hello! What the devil are you doing here?' asked Baker, with a start. Needless to say, he was looking at me.

But my fascinated eyes were upon the other person in the room. Certainly he suffered from a bad cold indeed, for despite the heat of the room his face was closely muffled, and his hat was pulled low on his brow. The disguise, however, was insufficient. I knew him even before Lavender had stepped forward and snatched the hat from his head.

'This, I take it, is your young friend of the bank?' inquired my friend.

I nodded, still staring.

'It is too bad that he has a cold,' said Lavender, replacing the ravished hat. The bank clerk was furious. 'Who are you?' he shrieked. 'What are you doing here?'

The first question was addressed to Lavender; the second to me. Suddenly the fellow ran for the door.

'It is locked!' said Dorrington evenly. 'Please sit down. If you will listen for a moment — '

'By what right am I locked in?' raved the young man with the cold. 'Open the door at once, or I shall send for the police.'

'Look here, Mason,' said Lavender. His voice stopped us all. 'If you really want trouble, all right. If you insist, we'll open the door. Inside of ten minutes, if we do, you will be under arrest charged with the theft of diamonds valued at $25,000. If you are willing to stay here and listen to what we have to say, your arrest may be a matter of months yet: that is, until your next venture into crime. What do you say?'

Suddenly the young man called Mason fell into a chair. He pointed a shaking finger at the white-faced Baker.

'He did it!' he squeaked. 'He did it! I'll swear on a cross, gentlemen, he did it!'

4

It was a merry party that gathered about Mrs. Baker's table, that evening, for the special dinner that my excellent landlady had insisted upon preparing. Lavender, of course, was the guest of honor, and I never had seen him in better form, conversationally. His talk was alternately brilliant and absurd; he turned from sobriety to nonsense, and back again, as night falls in the tropics — that is, with no intermediate period of twilight. He kept the table in an uproar, while I — an oyster, socially — sat mute, with beaming, idiotic countenance. All I cared to do that evening was to admire Lavender and laugh at his sallies. My worship must have irritated him, for I found myself the butt of more than half his jests.

I sat at his left, and Dorrington at his right. The others at the table were Mr. and Mrs. Henry Baker. The latter had learned the truth from me, and in the recital I did not spare her husband. And Henry Baker as he sat at table was a chastened individual.

When the memorable night was spent, and Lavender was smoking a farewell cigar with Dorrington and me, before seeking his rooms, the subdued Baker put in a tardy appearance in Mrs. Baker's astonishing plush parlor. He was embarrassed, but apparently he had his instructions. He came directly at Lavender with outstretched hand.

'I just want to say that, of course, I'm very much obliged to you,' he said, with some attempt at dignity.

'Oh, that's all right,' smiled Lavender. 'Glad to be of service. I ought to say though, Baker, that what I did was for your wife's sake, not for yours. You were in a rather tight place for a time, and now that you're well out of it I hope you'll be more careful.'

Mr. Baker muttered in his mustache. He was understood to repeat that he was very grateful, and he added that he would not be found in trouble again. Something was bothering him apparently. At length he came out with it.

'Has Mason confessed?'

'Yes,' said Lavender. 'Mason confessed to me this afternoon. He was given a chance to tell the truth and be given his freedom, and at first he refused. He was certain he could fasten the theft on you. I told him very frankly that I had a small opinion of your moral perceptions myself, and that if it were money that had been taken I should have had no hesitation in suspecting you. I also told him that I did not believe your nerve was equal to the diamond job. And besides, you knew nothing about them; you even tried to sell them to the man from whom they had been stolen.'

Mr. Baker looked extremely foolish throughout this monologue.

'Do you mind telling me how he got them?' he asked, quite humbly.

'Not at all,' said Lavender. 'In a nutshell, this is what happened: Dorrington placed the diamonds in your wife's strong box for safe-keeping, something over two weeks ago; then he left town. The safe was open and Mrs. Baker, with her back to it, was writing out a deposit slip, preparatory to sending Maude Image to the bank with the day's receipts. The money which was to go to the bank also was in the safe — on the shelf next to the package of diamonds. The small change was wrapped in the paper wrappers furnished for that purpose, so that there were several small packages of about the same size as that containing the diamonds.

'Mrs Baker asked Maude Image to give her the money on the shelf. Maude Image, who is so near-sighted that she can hardly see, promptly picked out and gave her everything within reach, including the package of diamonds. Your wife put them into the bag with the money, gave the bag to the Image, and that was the last of the diamonds so far as Dorrington was concerned, until he saw them this morning. Needless to add, they were received with the money by your friend Mason, who leaped to the correct conclusion that there had been a mistake. He held them for a few days; then as there was no outcry he determined to keep and dispose of them. He needed money.

'He had to find a purchaser and so chose you, Mr. Baker, as his agent, thinking that if there were trouble he would blame the whole affair on you. He very nearly succeeded, as you know. If he had been an ideal thief, he would have investigated the ownership of the diamonds, but he slipped up; and of course he could not know that you would hustle off with them to the very man who owned them. No one knew Dorrington had lost the diamonds but Dorrington and myself; I had warned him to make no popular outcry. The result of his silence was Mason's attempt to sell the gems, and your offer of them to Dorrington. Is that clear?'

'One moment, Lavender,' I broke in. 'Why should Mason have gone to Mr. Baker with the diamonds in the first place?'

'He owed Baker money,' said Lavender, with a glance at the man before him. 'He also owed Baker a grudge. It was on Baker's tip that Mason lost money and got himself in Baker's debt. Eh, Baker?'

Baker had the grace to blush.

'I'm sorry about Mason,' he muttered. 'Honest I am. What did you do with him?'

'I let him off with a warning. It seems that some inkling of his trouble had reached the bank, and he was discharged yesterday. I saw no reason for adding to his misery — particularly as you were very much to blame in the matter. I should like to repeat my warning to you.'

Mr. Baker smiled feebly and slunk out of the room. Lavender laughed.

'Still a bit of a cur,' he observed. 'His wife sent him in here to thank me, of course. But it has turned out very well. Now she has the upper hand, and I think Henry will be kept rigidly to the chalk line from this time on. If he ever slips, Gilly, let me know.'

The Mid-Watch Tragedy

1

The military-looking gentleman produced a thin, expensive watch from his waistcoat pocket, and put it away again.

'The bar,' said he sagely, 'will be open in half an hour.'

I acquiesced with a smile. He flicked the end of his cigarette overboard and idly watched its descent until a wave took it. Then, as if the action had removed a weight from his mind, he turned briskly and continued. 'Do you play bridge, Mr. Gilruth?'

'No,' I said thankfully, 'I don't.'

Where the devil, I wondered, had he got my name? We had been hardly an hour at sea. He was excessively friendly — much as, I understood, were the professional gamblers against whom the company had thoughtfully warned its passengers.

'My wife will be disappointed,' said he. 'You and your friend are about the only eligibles she and her sister have discovered to date. I can play — but I won't.'

I resented his easy assumptions. My acquaintance with Jimmy Lavender had not been without its practical value, and I had learned to distrust plausible strangers.

'That, I believe, is my friend's situation, also,' I replied stiffly. 'However, he must answer for himself.'

'Of course,' said he with a courteous nod. 'My respects to him, please. His reputation is well-known to me. My name is Rittenhouse,' he added, handing me his card. 'And now I must run along and see what has become of my women.'

He turned away, and I watched him for a moment as he threaded the crowded deck before I, too, turned and went in search of Lavender. It was Lavender's vacation, I mused, and I was in a sense his nurse — at any rate, his companion — and I did not intend that he should be bothered, if I could prevent. Not that Lavender was ill, but certainly he was tired; and even if the plausible Mr. Rittenhouse were not a professional gambler, bridge was no game for a man who needed rest.

I circled the promenade deck in my search and at length climbed to the boat deck, just in time to see Lavender appear at the top of the aft companionway, closely followed by a deck steward dragging a couple of chairs. The detective indicated a spot amidships, somewhat sheltered, and balanced on either side by giant air funnels.

'Dump 'em down here,' he ordered. 'Hullo, Gilly! This looks like as good a place as any. A quiet spot on the aft boat deck is always to be preferred to the chatter and publicity of the promenade. I'm sick of crowds!'

'See anybody you know?' I asked casually.

'Nary soul,' said he, 'and don't want to. I've seen the purser, however, and the dining room steward. We're to sit at the purser's table — all men. It's rough on you, Gilly, but I haven't enough small talk to be good company for the women.'

'There are two of them looking for you,' I said grimly, and told him of my meeting with Rittenhouse, at whose card until that moment I had not troubled to look. It revealed that the military — looking man's name was Joseph, and that he was a Major, retired, in the United States Marine Corps.

Lavender snatched the card, as if to verify my assertions, then chuckled delightedly.

'By George!' he cried. 'It's Rit!'

'You know him, then?' I asked somewhat taken aback.

'Know him! Why we've hunted men together! He served two terms as police commissioner of Los Angeles, where I met him. A better man never held office. And you thought he was a crook!' He chuckled again with great happiness. 'Where is he?'

'Looking for his wife and her sister, I believe.'

'I must hunt him up. I hope you weren't rude, Gilly! Anybody else of interest on board?'

'I've looked over the passenger list,' I replied airily. 'There's a British lord — Denbigh, I think; a Sir John

Rutherford; Betty Cosgrave, the screen actress; an Italian baroness whose name I forget, and the Rev. Henry Murchison of Cedar Rapids, Iowa.'

'Good!' laughed Lavender. 'You have them pat. The baroness, I fancy, is the dark woman who looked me over carefully as I came on board. She was standing at the rail, and I thought she looked as if she knew me, or believed she did. She looked Italian, anyway, and she was romantic enough looking to be a baroness. I thought for a moment that she was going to speak to me, but if she was she thought better of it.'

'Confound it, Jimmy,' I said, 'I hope you're not going to be bothered by baronesses or Majors, or Majors' wives, on this trip; or Majors' wives' sisters, either. Your nerves are all shot to pieces.'

'And you are an idiot,' was the amused reply. 'However, I'll promise not to play bridge.'

'It would be just our luck to blunder onto trouble of some sort,' I went on morosely. 'Jimmy, if anybody robs the ship's safe, you are not to interfere. Let the Major run down the thief, since he's such a good man.'

He laughed again. 'All right,' said he, 'I'll go and see him about it now.' And off he went, to hunt up his erstwhile crony, the retired Major and man-hunter, whom, I suspect, he discovered in the smoking-room (which was also the drinking-room), for the bar had been open for several minutes.

And that is the way it all started, the memorable voyage of the trans-Atlantic liner, *Dianthus*, which added laurels to the reputation of my friend Lavender, and began his vacation in a manner — from Lavender's point of view — highly satisfying and successful.

Actually, it was the evening of the second day at sea that the first whisper of the trouble I had predicted reached our ears. My sardonic prophecy, however, was not accurate in its detail. The ship's safe — if it carried one — remained unmolested.

The day had been warm enough, but the evening called for wraps. The promenade deck was a scene of some activity, what with the hustling stewards and the eternally tramping Britons, who toiled around the oval like athletes training on a track. An Englishman is never happy unless he is walking or sitting before his fireplace; and the ship had no fireplaces. The boat deck, however, was comparatively deserted, and Lavender and I, wrapped in our rugs, looked out into the windy darkness and smoked contentedly. Our nearest companions were a spooning couple some yards away, half hidden by funnels, and wrapped in blankets and their own emotions. Major Rittenhouse, a likeable fellow, as I had rapidly discovered, had surrendered at discretion, and was playing the amiable martyr in the card room.

An occasional steward drifted past, and once the second officer of the ship stopped for a word and a cigarette, but for the most part we were left to ourselves.

'Indeed,' said I, 'I believe we have the choice of locations, Lavender.' And at that instant the Italian baroness hove into view.

Her name, we had discovered, was Borsolini — the Baroness Borsolini. She came forward uncertainly, wavered in passing, passed on, and in a few moments came back. She was quite alone, and obviously she wished to speak to us. On the third trip she had made up her mind, and came swiftly to our side.

'You are Mr. Lavender?' she murmured. 'I must speak with you. May I sit down?'

'Of course,' said my friend, and rose to his feet to assist her. 'Something is worrying you, I fear.'

'You are right,' said the baroness. 'I am very much afraid.'

Her English was perfect. Her manner was pretty and appealing.

'Something has frightened you?' asked Lavender encouragingly.

She bent forward and studied his face closely in the darkness.

'You are a good man,' she said at length. 'I can tell. I think you are a poet.'

Lavender squirmed and feebly gesticulated. Before he could deny the amazing charge, she had hurried on.

'Yes, I am afraid. Last night — after I had retired — someone was in my cabin!'

'A thief?'

The words came eagerly from the detective's lips. In his interest, he forgot her preposterous notion about his profession.

'I think so. But nothing was taken away. He did not find what he sought.'

Lavender's interest deepened. 'What did he seek?' he asked.

'My jewels,' said the baroness. 'What else?'

'They are valuable then?'

'They are very valuable, my friend. They are valuable because it would cost a fortune to replace them; but they are priceless because they are my family jewels. I speak of replacing them, but believe me, they could not be replaced.'

My friend's cap came off to the breeze. 'Tell me how you know there was someone in your cabin,' he said.

'I awoke suddenly — I don't know why I awoke. I suppose I felt someone there. There were little sounds in the room

— soft, brushing sounds — and breathing. Light, so light, I could scarcely catch it. It was only for an instant, then the man was gone. I must have made some little sound myself that alarmed him. As he went, I almost saw him — you understand? He seemed to glide through the door, which he had to open to escape. He made no sound, and what I saw was just black against gray as the door opened. I only half saw him — the other half I felt. You understand?'

'Yes,' said Lavender, 'I understand perfectly. But how can you be sure it was a man? Probably it was — but are you sure?'

'I think so — that is all. It is my feeling that tells me it was a man. I cannot explain — but if it had been a woman, I think I should have known.'

Lavender nodded. 'No doubt you are right,' he said. 'Whom have you told of this, Baroness?'

'I have told no one but yourselves. You will advise me whom I should tell?'

'You had better tell Mr. Crown, the purser. He will, if he thinks best, tell the captain, I suppose, or whoever handles investigations of this sort. At any rate, Mr. Crown is the man to whom the first report should be made. I am sure he will do whatever is necessary. Probably he will have his own way of getting at the man who did this. I would see the purser at once, Baroness, if I were you.'

She rose promptly. 'Thank you. I am sure your advice is good. I shall go to Mr. Crown at once. You are very good.'

'Meanwhile,' said Lavender, 'we shall, of course, say nothing. Good night, Baroness, and I hope you will not be disturbed again.'

We rose with her, and watched her as she tripped away to the companionway. With a wave of her hand, she descended the steps and vanished. Lavender shoved me down into my chair.

'Stay here, Gilly,' he said. 'I'll be back shortly.'

A moment later he, too, had disappeared in the direction of the lower deck.

Well, it had come! My unthinking prophecy had borne fruit, and Lavender already was involved. Where would it end?

I lay back in my deck chair and earnestly consigned the baroness and her family jewels to perdition. It occurred to me that it had been nothing less than criminal for her to come on board our ship with the infernal things. She could just as well have waited for the *Maltania*! And Lavender might then have been allowed to have his vacation in peace.

In ten minutes, the subject of my paternal flutterings was back.

'She went, all right,' said he laconically.

'I should hope she would,' I retorted. 'Did you think she wouldn't?'

'I wanted to be sure, Gilly,' answered Lavender kindly. 'I'm wondering why she didn't go to the purser first; why she singled me out for her attention; why she didn't put her blessed jewels in the purser's charge when she came on board — it's the thing to do. I'm also wondering how she knows me. For I'm convinced that she does know me, in spite of her assertion that I was singled out because I look like a 'good man.' I am more than ever convinced that she recognized me when I came on board. She wanted to speak to me then, although she had no attempted jewel robbery to report yesterday. Really, it's all very interesting.'

'Yes,' I admitted, 'it is. Do you think there will be another attempt, Jimmy?'

'I wouldn't be surprised,' said he thoughtfully. 'In fact, I would almost bet on it.'

2

In the dining saloon, the next morning, the company had perceptibly thinned out, for a stiff breeze and a choppy sea had sprung up in the night. At the purser's table, however, we sat six strong, as we had begun the voyage. Crown, the purser, pink complexioned and almost ridiculously fat, beamed good nature upon his charges, from his seat at the head of the table. He was in jovial spirits.

'If there were a prize offered for the table that showed no desertions,' said he with a chuckle, 'I think we should win.'

Beverley of Toronto, who sat at my left, growled humorously. 'There are several days ahead of us,' he significantly observed. 'I, for one, do not intend to crow.'

Lavender, who had been the last one to sit down, was looking around the room. The Major's wife, thinking him to be looking in her direction, raised her brows and smiled, and he caught the gesture and smiled and nodded back. He spoke to the purser, beside whom he sat.

'Two of the notables have not materialized,' he remarked casually. 'The baroness and the clergyman are missing.'

The purser looked startled.

'Yes,' he answered, 'I noticed that. Murchison is ill, I hear; but I don't understand the baroness' absence. She looked to me like a sailor.'

He seemed worried for a moment, and looked back at Lavender as if longing to confide in him; but the presence of the others at the table prevented. Lavender himself, having given the officer the hint he intended, devoted himself to his breakfast. From time to time, however, during the progress of the meal, he glanced toward the baroness' seat at a neighboring table, as if hoping to see that it had been occupied during the moments of his inattention. But the breakfast hour passed away and the object of his solicitude did not appear. The purser, too, continued to be worried, although he kept up a lively flow of conversation.

Outside the saloon door, the detective and the ship's officer paused while the passengers dispersed.

'She may be ill, of course,' said the purser, at length. It was almost humorously obvious that he would have been relieved to hear that the baroness was very ill indeed.

'Of course,' agreed Lavender, 'but we had better find out. She told you, I suppose, that she came to me first?'

'Yes,' said the purser, 'one of my assistants tried to look after her, but she insisted on seeing me. I'm glad she was so cautious about it. Usually, a woman gets excited, tells everybody her difficulties, and then in loud tones demands to see the captain. As a result, the trouble — whatever it is — is all over the ship in no time, and everybody is nervous. I suppose I'm a fool, Mr. Lavender, but somehow I'm nervous now, myself. I hope there's no further trouble.'

'What did you do, last night?'

'Spoke to the night watchman. He's supposed to have had an eye on her cabin all night. Of course, he couldn't watch it every minute, and do the rest of his work, too; but he was ordered to notice it particularly every time he passed, and to hang around a bit each time. I fancy he did it; he's a good man.'

'And the baroness herself?'

'Refused, in spite of all my persuasion, to place her jewels in charge of my office. Of course, in the circumstances, if anything does happen to them, it's her own lookout. Just the same; that sort of thing, if it gets out, gives a ship a black eye, so to speak.'

'Well,' said Lavender, 'we'd better have a look at her cabin. Nobody seems to be interested in our movements. Come on, Gilly!' He started up the stairs to the cabin deck. 'Who is her stewardess, Purser?'

'Mrs. King, a nice old soul. I spoke to her, too, but all I said was that the baroness was nervous, and to do what she could for her. We'll see Mrs. King at once.'

He sighed and rolled heavily away, and we followed closely at his heels, down the corridors of the lurching vessel to the stewardesses' sitting room. Mrs. King, however, had nothing to tell us.

'She didn't call,' said the woman, 'and I didn't go near her.'

'She wasn't down to breakfast this morning,' explained the purser, 'and we thought perhaps she was ill. You haven't been to her cabin yet, this morning?'

'No, sir,' replied Mrs. King, 'having had the lady's own orders not to wake her if she didn't choose to get up.'

'I see. Well, you must go to her now, and see if she needs you. She may be ill, or she may just have missed the breakfast gong and be sleeping. Give her my compliments, and say that I was inquiring for her.'

The woman seemed reluctant, and hung back for a moment; then she moved slowly off to the door of the cabin numbered B.12, where she paused uncertainly.

'All right,' said the purser impatiently, 'knock, and then go in!'

Mrs. King timidly knocked, and again stopped as if in apprehension.

'What's the matter?' asked Lavender, in

his friendliest tones, seeing that the woman was frightened.

The ship lurched heavily, lay over for a long moment, and came up again. We all braced our legs and clung to the nearest woodwork.

'She doesn't — answer,' said the matron faintly.

'Open the door!' ordered the purser.

Thus adjured, Mrs. King turned the handle, and with a terrific effort put her head inside the door. In an instant the head was withdrawn. The woman's face was pale and scared. The purser looked angry. Lavender, however, knew what had happened. With a quick frown, he pushed past the motionless woman and entered the little cabin, the purser and I at his heels. We filled the place.

There was no particular disorder. The port stood half open, as it had stood through the night, to allow ventilation. On the upholstered wall bench stood the baroness' bags. Her trunk half projected from beneath the bunk. The curtains blew gently with a soft, swishing sound.

Even in the bunk itself there was small

disorder. Yet beneath the white coverings, with tossed hair and distorted features, the Baroness Borsolini lay dead.

For an instant, we all stood in silence. Then, from the corridor without, sounded the frightened whimper of Mrs. King, the stewardess. Lavender beckoned her inside, and she docilely obeyed.

'Stay here until we have finished,' he quietly ordered.

'Good God!' said Crown, the purser, in awed dismay. Then he continued to stare, without speech, at the bed.

Lavender bent over the silent figure of the woman who, only the night before, had whispered her trouble to him.

'Strangled,' he murmured softly. 'Killed without a sound.'

'Good God!' said the purser again.

Once more the stewardess' scared whimper sounded.

'Don't, please,' said my friend, gently. To me, he said, 'Gilly, can you say how long she has been dead?'

Anticipating the question, I had been examining the body, although without touching it. Now I stepped forward for a closer examination.

'Six or seven hours, at least,' I said at length. 'The ship's doctor — Brown — will tell you better than I.'

'We'd better have him in,' said Lavender, 'although you are probably right. Excuse me, Mr. Crown,' he added. 'I don't mean to usurp your position in this matter.'

The purser shuddered. 'Go ahead,' he said. 'I'll be glad to do whatever you suggest.'

'Then get the doctor here, quietly, and ask Rittenhouse if he cares to come down. What else there is to do, you will know better than I — that is, I suppose you will have to report to the captain, or something of the sort. You'd better take Mrs. King out of this, too, Crown. I'd like to talk to her a little later, though.'

He looked keenly at the frightened, shaking woman, but his touch on her arm as he uttered his last words was gentle. I knew that he was wondering about her hesitation before opening the door. I, too, had been wondering. Was it merely a woman's uncanny prescience, or some-thing more significant?

When the purser and the matron had gone away, he turned to me.

'A queer, unhappy case, Gilly,' he quietly remarked. 'Do you sense it? The beginning, if I am not mistaken, of something very curious indeed.'

Without further words, he turned from the bed and began a swift search of the cabin. His nimble fingers flew as he worked, and under his touch the posses-sions of the murdered baroness came to view and disappeared again with skillful method. Apparently he found nothing to guide him.

When he had finished, he said, 'The question is, of course: did he, or she, or they — whichever may have been the case — find what they were looking for?'

'The jewels are gone?' I asked. 'You didn't find them?'

'They are not here,' he replied, 'unless they are very cleverly hidden. The second question we are bound to consider, Gilly, is: were there any jewels?'

That startled me.

He continued, 'We have no proof that she ever had any jewels. She was vague enough about them, when she spoke to us — vague about their value — and she refused to deposit them with the purser, which was her proper course. We have only her word for it that she possessed the jewels, and that she carried them with her. None the less,' he added firmly, 'she may have had them, and they may have been stolen. Certainly she was not murdered as a matter of whim.'

'I think you suspect something that you are not mentioning, Jimmy,' I remarked, with another glance at the dead woman.

He followed the glance. 'Yes,' he replied, 'you are right. I believe this all began somewhere on shore. Almost the most important thing to be done, is to establish the identity of this woman.'

'You doubt that she is — ?'

'The Baroness Borsolini? Well, yes and no. She may have been just what she claimed to be, and yet nobody in particular. Baroness, in Italy, means nothing of importance. The last Italian baron I knew was floorwalker in a

Chicago department store. And, of course, she may not have been a baroness at all. My doubt of the poor woman, I will admit, goes back to the fact that she seemed to know me. However, if we are fortunate, we shall know all about her before long.'

Again I looked a question.

'Last night,' said he, 'I sent a wireless, in code, to Inspector Gallery, in New York. I was curious about the baroness and her tale, and suspecting further trouble, I tried to anticipate some of our difficulties.'

'You anticipated — this?'

'No,' he flared quickly. 'Not this, by Heaven! If I had, Gilly, I'd have stood guard myself all night long. I anticipated another attempt on the jewels,' he added in lower tones. 'Another attempt on whatever it is this woman had that her murderer wanted. We must have a talk with that night watchman, too, before long. I wonder who occupied the cabin across the way?'

'We can soon discover that,' said I; and at that moment the purser came back with the doctor.

Brown, a fussy little man with a beard the color of his name, had heard the story from the purser, and was prepared for what he saw. He conducted a swift and skillful examination that proved his ability, and verified my statement as to the time the woman had been dead.

'Let us assume seven hours, then,' said Lavender. 'That would fix the murder at about two in the morning — possibly a little earlier, possibly a little later. Where the devil would the watchman have been at that hour? No doubt he had just passed on, for certainly the murderer would have been watching for him. By the way, Crown, who occupies B.14?'

The baroness' cabin was at the corner of an intersecting passage, and its entrance was off the smaller corridor. B.14 occupied the corresponding position across the passage, and was the opposite cabin to which Lavender had referred.

'I'll find out for you,' answered the purser; but the doctor replied to the question.

'A clergyman,' he said. 'Murchison, of some place in Iowa. He's ill. He had me in, last night.'

'Last night?' echoed my friend.

'Yes,' said the doctor, 'and it can't have been very long before — before this happened! About one o'clock, I think. It's not nice to think that this may even have been going on, while I was just across the way.'

'How is he?'

'Oh, he's sick enough, but it's the usual thing. It was new to him, though, and I suppose he thought he was going to die. The poor chap is pretty low.'

'He may have heard something, if he was awake,' suggested Lavender. 'Can he be questioned?'

'Oh, yes, but I doubt if he heard anything but his own groans. Somebody's with him now. I heard talking as I came by.'

'I told Major Rittenhouse,' volunteered the purser. 'He said he'd be right down. He ought to have been here by this time.'

'We'd better go to my stateroom,' said Lavender. 'There's nothing further to be learned here, I think. I shall want to talk with the night watchman, Purser, when I can get to him. I suppose he's asleep now.

Doctor Brown, would you care to speak to your patient across the way? Ask him if he heard anything in the night, you know; and press the point. Any trifle may be important.'

The door opened and the tall figure of Major Rittenhouse entered softly. He closed the door quietly behind him.

'I heard the last question,' he remarked, then glanced at the bed. For just an instant, his eyes rested on the dead woman, then without emotion he continued. 'I've already questioned Mr. Murchison, Lavender. It occurred to me as a good idea to look up the nearest neighbor. In a case like this, time is of considerable importance. Murchison was awake most of the night, and had the doctor in, once. About four o'clock he got up and staggered around his room a bit, then opened his door. He saw someone leaving this cabin, and supposed the baroness to be ill, too, for he thought no more about it.'

'Four o'clock!' cried Lavender. 'And if he thought the baroness was ill, he must have seen — '

'Mrs. King!' gasped the purser, with

new horror in his voice.

'I don't know her name, and neither did Murchison,' said Rittenhouse; 'but the woman he saw was one of the stewardesses.'

3

Rain fell heavily throughout the afternoon, filling the smoke-rooms and lounges of the floating hotel with animated conversation; but in Lavender's stateroom, as the great liner shouldered through the squall, a grimmer conversation went forward, unknown to the hundreds of our fellow passengers. It was feared that, soon enough, the ill tidings of death would spread through the ship, and throw a blight over the happy voyagers. Meanwhile, the task of apprehending the murderer of the unfortunate baroness had to move swiftly. It is probable that no shipboard mystery ever occurred more fortuitously; that is to say, with two more admirable detectives than Lavender and Rittenhouse actually on board to handle the investigation; but it is equally probable that no more mysterious affair ever engaged the talents of either investigator. We were a little world of our own, isolated from the rest of civilization by hundreds of miles of salt water; our inhabitants were comparatively few in number, and there was no opportunity whatever of escape. Somewhere in our midst actually moved and ate and slept a man or a woman guilty of a hideous crime of violence; yet not a single clue apparently existed to the identity of that individual, unless Murchison's testimony had supplied it.

Mrs. King, the stewardess, was reluctant to an extraordinary degree, when for the second time she was questioned about her murdered charge. At first, she denied pointblank any knowledge of the events of the night, then, as Lavender continued to probe, she burst into a storm of hysterical weeping. Confronted with the purport of the clergyman's information, she made a statement that only added mystery to the case.

'I did go in there at four o'clock,' she said tearfully, addressing the purser, 'and, so help me God, Mr. Crown, she was already dead!'

The purser's astonished glance went round the cabin and settled on my friend;

but Lavender only nodded.

'That is what you should have told us at once,' he said. 'You were afraid of compromising yourself, but you only compromised yourself more deeply by keeping silent. You see, Rit,' he continued, turning to the Major, 'the time element remains unconfused. The murder occurred at about two o'clock, as the body indicated. Now, Mrs. King, let us have no more evasions and no more denials. If you stick to the truth, no harm will come to you that you don't deserve. Tell us exactly why you went to the baroness' cabin at four o'clock in the morning.'

'She — she called me!' whispered the woman, in a voice so low that we caught the words only with difficulty.

'That, of course, is nonsense,' said Lavender, severely; but Major Ritten-house had caught a glimpse of the truth.

'You mean that the call board showed a call from her room,' he interrupted. 'But you didn't hear the bell ring, did you?'

The woman shook her head.

'She was probably asleep, Jimmy,' continued the Major. 'She didn't hear the bell, but when she awoke, some hours after it had rung, the board showed the baroness' number up. She answered — and found the body!'

'Is that what happened?' demanded Lavender of the woman.

Again Mrs. King responded with a gesture of the head, this time affirmative. The purser was angry.

'You are the night stewardess,' he cried. 'You have no right to be asleep.'

'Nevertheless,' said Lavender, 'she was asleep. It doesn't help matters now to scold her. What happened is this: the murderer entered the cabin about two o'clock, and the baroness woke — possibly she had not been asleep. She heard the intruder, and sat up. Before she could scream, his hands were at her throat. There was a struggle, sharp but brief, and somehow the victim managed to reach and touch the call button. The ringing of the bell in the passage alarmed the murderer and he fled. Mrs. King was asleep and did not get the call. Two hours later, she awoke, saw that a call had come from the baroness' cabin, and responded.

Murchison, across the way, opened his door and saw her leaving the room. A pity he didn't open his door at two o'clock!'

Rittenhouse nodded and took up the quiz.

'You saw nothing in the room when you entered?' he asked. 'Nothing that would give you an idea as to who did this thing?'

'No,' answered the woman faintly.

'Was there a light in the room?' She shook her head.

'Then how did you know the baroness was dead?'

'I — I turned on the light.'

'Why did you turn on the light?'

'She had called me,' answered the woman, somewhat defiantly. 'I spoke when I went in, and she didn't answer. I thought maybe she had got up and gone out — I thought maybe she was ill. So I turned on the light, and then I saw — I saw her!' Rittenhouse nodded again.

'And then you turned out the light, and went away?' Lavender finished. 'Why didn't you tell somebody what had happened?'

'I was afraid,' said Mrs. King simply. 'I was afraid they would think I had done it.'

'Hm-m!' said Lavender. He looked at the Major, who shrugged his shoulders.

'I guess that's all, Purser,' said Lavender, at length. 'Let's have the night watchman in.'

But John Dover, the night watchman, an ex-sergeant of the British army, could tell nothing. His story was straightforward enough.

'Yes, sir,' said he frankly. 'He passed that room many times, sir. There was no trouble that he could see, sir, at any time. If there 'ad been, He'd 'ave looked into it. There was no light in the room, sir, at any time.'

This, after an hour's questioning, was still his story.

'It's probably quite true, too,' observed Lavender, when the man had been cautioned to keep his mouth shut, and had been dismissed. 'The murderer wouldn't be fool enough to attract the watchman. Well, Rit, where are we?'

'Just about where we began, Jimmy, I

'should say,' answered the Major.

'You believe the stewardess' story?' asked the purser dubiously.

'There's no earthly reason to disbelieve it, as yet,' frankly responded Lavender. 'She could have done it, I suppose, but so could a dozen others. Extraordinary as her statement is, it has many of the earmarks of truth. I believe she did exactly what eight out of ten women would have done in the circumstances. We can't leave her out of our calculations, of course, but certainly we must allow her to believe that we accept her story in toto. In point of fact, I do accept it.'

It was not long after these developments that tidings of the death of the Baroness Borsolini were all over the ship. Exactly how the news was started, nobody knew, for everybody with direct knowledge had been sworn to secrecy. It is a difficult thing, however, to hush up as serious a matter as murder, particularly on shipboard; and no doubt the leak could have been traced to the night watchman or Mrs. King, or the clergyman of the ship's doctor, or possibly even to the Major's wife or her sister. It is not the sort of knowledge one human being can possess without telling to another.

The purser, Crown, was deeply annoyed, for he was worried about the good name of the ship; but Lavender only grunted and said it could not be helped. As a matter of strict accuracy, it was the very revelation of the murder that brought us one of our strongest and strangest clues. It brought to Lavender's stateroom, the Hon. Arthur Russell, of Beddington, Herts., England, son of that Lord Denbigh whose name I had discovered on the ship's passenger list.

⋆ ⋆ ⋆

All over the ship the rumor of tragedy flew, once it had started, and the passengers gathered in groups to discuss the fearsome occurrence. In the smoking-rooms, the male passengers bragged and told each other what they would do to apprehend the murderer, and in the lounges the women twittered and hissed like the gaudy birds of passage that they were. Many were frankly alarmed at the thought that the assassin was still at large, walking among them. They stated their fears audibly, and the purser was stormed by brigades of them, seeking information and assurances of safety.

'We may all be murdered in our beds,' said they, in effect, so vehemently and in such numbers that Crown probably wished in his heart that many of them would be.

'Idiots!' said Lavender to me in privacy after the harassed purser had told him what was going on. 'They are, if anything, safer than before. The murder of the baroness was not a result of blood-lust, nor the beginning of wholesale assassination. The selected victim has been killed, and for the murderer the episode is over. Quite the last thing he would do, unless he is crazy, is kill someone else. What he wants to do now is keep himself a secret, not to advertise himself by further crime. People are funny, Gilly; they don't think. Most murderers are really very safe men to be near, after they have committed their murder. They have it out of their system; their hate or their vengeance has been satisfied; the one who stood in their path has been removed, and in all probability they will never again commit that crime. The way to stop murder — philosophically speaking — is not to lock up or kill murderers, but to prevent the accomplishment of crime, or even the desire to kill, by scientific, educational methods. This, however,' he added, with a smile and a shrug, 'is not a doctrine that I often preach, and never in public. It would land me in the insane asylum!'

I was inclined to agree with his last assertion; but Lavender is a queer fellow, and his philosophy, as he states it, is very plausible. I merely smiled politely, and at his suggestion rang the bell and asked that our tardy luncheon be sent to the stateroom. As it happened, the Hon. Arthur Russell came in with the tray — that is, he was hard on the heels of the waiter who bore it, and he apologized profusely for interrupting. He was a mannerly young Briton, handsome and likeable, and we asked him to sit down and have a cup of tea.

I supposed him to be spokesman for his father, or for some group of the passengers, but his mission, it developed, was quite a different one. He was not seeking information; he had it to impart.

'I say, Mr. Lavender,' he began, 'is it all true, this that I hear? That the Baroness Borsolini is dead?'

'Yes,' replied my friend, 'quite true. She was found dead in her berth, this morning.'

'And that she was' — he boggled over the word 'murdered,' and substituted another one — 'that she was killed?'

'Yes,' said Lavender again. 'There is not a doubt in the world that she was murdered, Mr. Russell.'

'Good Lord!' said the boy. He drew a long breath. 'That's what everybody is saying. I couldn't believe it!'

'Why?'

'Because — well, I couldn't, that's all! It seemed too horrible. Why, only last night, sir, she was with me on deck — full of life — and happy — why, I may have been the last person to see her alive!' he finished.

'The individual who killed her was the last person to see her alive,' said Lavender coolly.

'Of course!' cried the boy. 'I didn't think of that. Say, that's clever!'

Lavender smiled a little, not displeased by the boy's quick admiration.

'I think perhaps you have something to tell us, Mr. Russell,' continued my friend. 'Don't hesitate, if you have. Any information is very welcome.'

The Hon. Arthur Russell gulped his tea, suddenly and convulsively, then put it aside.

'Well, I have!' said he. 'Not much — but I've got her address!'

'Her address?'

'Yes, sir. She gave it to me last night. You see, we had struck up an acquaintance, and we liked each other. We sat out on deck and talked, pretty late. I told her about my school life, and she told me a lot about America; and when we were parting, I said I'd like to write to her. So she gave me her address. Wrote it on a piece of paper and gave it to me. Here it is!'

With something of the air of a conjurer,

he produced the paper. His youthful face was alight with the excitement of his news, which he believed to be of the highest importance. He could have been no more than twenty, while the baroness had been all of thirty-five, although pretty enough. Apparently, the boy had been greatly smitten. It was rather amusing, and rather pitiful.

As he spoke, he handed Lavender the scrap of paper that he had taken from his pocket.

'That's it,' he concluded. 'Florence, Italy. The Hotel Caravan. That's her writing, sir!'

Lavender rose to his feet and carried the paper to the light. The boy too rose, and followed him. The interest of both was profound, although for the life of me I could see no reason for excitement in the discovery of the dead woman's address.

'Interesting,' commented my friend, at length. 'Very interesting indeed! And, if I'm not mistaken, very important, too. I'm really very much obliged to you, Mr. Russell.'

'I'm glad if it's a help,' said the boy,

flushing. His eyes sparkled. 'I'd like to think that I had — ' Suddenly he broke off, and his eyes bulged. 'Why,' he cried, 'you're looking at the wrong side!'

'No,' said Lavender, with a little smile, 'this is the right side. I saw the other side too, and it's interesting also — particularly as there is no Hotel Caravan in Florence, that I ever heard of. But it is the reverse that interests me most. You say that she took this paper out of her bag?'

'I didn't say so,' answered the boy accurately, 'but as a matter of fact, she did. Tore it off a large piece, and wrote on it. That's her handwriting!'

He was still stupefied by Lavender's curious action, and still certain that in a veritable specimen of the baroness' handwriting he had furnished us with a sensational clue. But Lavender continued to study the reverse of the fragment. At length, he handed it to me.

'What do you make of it, Gilly?' he asked.

I looked, and saw nothing but a fragment of what apparently had been a printed form of some kind, for there were upon it several words in small print, and a perforated upper edge. The words were quite meaningless, removed from their context. Above the small print, however, was the one word 'line' in larger type.

'A ship's form of some kind?' I hazarded. 'Torn from a book of similar forms?'

'Exactly,' agreed Lavender. 'The word 'Line,' of course, is the last word of 'Rodgers Line.' The rest, at the moment, means nothing. If we had the whole form, it might be very illuminating.'

There was a tap on the door, and a moment later Major Rittenhouse entered the stateroom.

'Jimmy,' said the newcomer, 'there's a message coming in for you, upstairs. One of the wireless boys just told me, and asked me to let you know. What've you got? Something new?'

'Yes,' said Lavender. 'What do you think of it, Rit?'

Rittenhouse turned the paper over in his fingers, and at the baroness' written name and address, he blinked.

'We are indebted to Mr. Russell for it,'

explained Lavender, and repeated the young Briton's story. 'But what do you make of the other side, Rit?'

After some cogitation, the Major made of it exactly what I had made.

'Well,' said Lavender, with a sigh, 'I may be wrong; but I thought I saw more than that.' His eyes narrowed. 'I'll tell you what, Rit,' he added suddenly, 'take it to your wife, or her sister, and ask either one what it is. I'll gamble that one of them will tell you.'

The Major appeared surprised.

'Are you joking, Lavender?' His tone was a bit indignant.

'Not a bit of it. I'm intensely serious. Will you do it?'

'Yes,' said Rittenhouse. 'I'll do anything you say, Jimmy; but I'm damned if I know what my wife has to do with this thing!'

'Meanwhile,' continued Lavender, 'let's see what New York has to report on the Baroness Borsolini. I've a feeling that another revelation is at hand.'

'May I come?' asked Arthur Russell eagerly.

'If you like,' smiled Lavender, 'but I'll

be right back. Better stay here, all of you. We don't want to parade about the ship in groups, and start a new set of rumors.'

He hurried away, and we sat back in our seats and impatiently awaited his return. In a few minutes he was back, with a small square of paper folded in his palm.

'Another interesting document,' he observed. 'This is Inspector Gallery's reply to my request for information concerning the baroness. It is in code, but I have translated it. Bear in mind, Rit, that he didn't know when he wired that the baroness was dead.'

He began to read the message.

'Baroness Borsolini probably Kitty Desmond, well-known adventuress and international character. If she has a small mole at left corner of mouth it is — '

'She has!' interrupted Arthur Russell, in high excitement.

'Yes,' said Lavender, 'she has.' He continued to read: ' — it is almost certain. Jewels probably famous Schuyler jewels, worth half million, stolen here two months ago. Have cabled Scotland Yard to meet you at Quarantine. Gallery.'

4

At the purser's table that evening, the murder of the Baroness Borsolini was the sole topic of conversation. We still sat six strong. Besides Lavender and I and the purser, there were Beverley of Toronto, Dudgeon of New York, and Isaacson of St. Louis. The latter three were acquainted with all the rumors, and they questioned Lavender and the purser diligently. That Lavender was a famous detective, and had been placed in charge of the case, was a piece of news that had circulated with the rest of the reports. Our fellow passengers at table felt themselves very fortunate indeed, to be so fortuitously placed with reference to the fountainheads of information, and I fancy they were vastly envied by passengers at the other tables. Throughout the meal, heads were turned constantly in our direction.

The rotund Crown, who, by virtue of his office, had been harassed even more than had Lavender, was inclined to be reticent and a bit short. Lavender merely smiled coldly, and replied with scrupulous accuracy to all questions leveled at him. The facts, he admitted without reserve, but he declined to indulge in speculation.

'It is obviously a case of a falling out of crooks,' he concluded. 'I have received a wireless message from New York, which positively identifies the baroness as a well-known and, if you like the term, a high class crook. The stolen jewels, if they have been stolen — and apparently they have been — are said to have originally disappeared in New York, some two months ago. I have no doubt that the baroness was on her way to Europe with them, and that the division of spoils was to be made there. Possibly she was to sell them. Her accomplices in the original theft, I should imagine, are for the most part on the way to Europe on other vessels. One, however, it would seem — or, any rate, somebody who knows the truth about the jewels — is on board this vessel. There is no cause for alarm. The decent passengers are quite safe.'

'She would have had to smuggle them in, wouldn't she?' asked Beverley of Toronto. The remark was more of a statement than a question.

'Yes,' replied Lavender, 'but that plan was probably worked out to the last comma. Smuggling offers no great difficulties to a clever person.'

At the close of the meal, we were surrounded by interested questioners; but not even the wiles of Betty Cosgrave, the screen star, could shake Lavender's reserve. We heartlessly left the purser to answer all interviewers, and hurried on deck. On the way up, we passed the captain, a pleasant-faced Englishman somewhat past middle life. He had something on his mind.

'Er — Mr. Lavender,' he observed, 'Mr. Crown has been keeping me informed, of course, of this extraordinary business. Nasty — very nasty indeed! Sinister! Mr. Crown, of course, acts for me and for the company. I have no wish to interfere with what is in better hands than my own; but you will understand that I am deeply affected by it all. May I ask whether you anticipate a — a successful conclusion?'

'Entirely successful, Captain Rogers,' replied Lavender seriously. 'It is the sort of case the very simplicity of which makes it difficult; but I believe it is yielding to treatment. I believe, quite honestly, that before long I shall be able to present you with the murderer of the Baroness Borsolini, and to turn over the stolen jewels.'

'Thank you,' said the captain with a nod. 'I have every confidence in you. And in Major Rittenhouse, too. Crown tells me you are both quite famous men in your field. I am sorry I could not have you at my table. If I can be of service, please command me.'

We finished our journey to the boat deck, without further interruption, and found our long unused deck chairs awaiting us. The night had cleared, but a cold breeze was blowing over the sea, and we wrapped ourselves in rugs to our chins. 'You seem pretty confident of success, Jimmy,' I ventured, when our pipes were going strongly, and the moment seemed propitious.

'I am confident,' said he. 'It is beyond credence that this fellow can escape. I am working privately on an idea of my own that, I confess, may not work out; but it looks promising. Frankly, Gilly, it has to do with that fragment of paper that the baroness gave young Russell; but that is all I dare say about it, at present. And I will ask you to keep that much a secret. What I want, of course, is the other piece of the paper — the larger piece.'

'Did Mrs. Rittenhouse identify it?' I asked curiously.

'She did,' replied my friend, almost grimly. 'She identified it in a moment, because both she and her sister have papers exactly like it. Rit is working with me in this, and I may hear from him at any minute. He is less of a figure than I, in this thing, and can snoop about with less attention.'

He sat in silence for a few moments, listening to the throb of the ship's great engines, and the rush of water beyond the white line of the rail.

Then I spoke again.

'Gallery was a bit previous, wasn't he, Jimmy, in cabling Scotland Yard to help you?'

'No, it was all right,' replied my friend, with a little smile. 'Don't be jealous, Gilly. I know exactly why Gallery did that. He thought that I might, at the last moment, feel some embarrassment in using the wireless; that is, that I might find myself in a position where I could not use it without betraying my suspicions, whatever they might be, to the person suspected. He anticipates that my use of the ship's wireless, if my actions are being watched — and, rest assured, they are being watched — may alarm the murderer. It was a piece of clear thinking on Gallery's part, a resourceful man's safeguard against chance or probability.'

I nodded, and again we sat without speech, until a step sounded along the boards, and the tall figure of the Major hove in view. Rittenhouse seated himself without a word beyond a greeting, and for a few moments we all smoked in silence.

'Murchison is still ill,' he said, 'but he's coming around. I've seen him again. He has nothing to add to his first statement. He saw no one but the stewardess last night; he is willing to swear to that. I've had another whirl at Dover, the watchman, too. He now remembers seeing the doctor leave Murchison's cabin. The incident made no impression on him, and he didn't think of it before; it was just a part of routine to him, to see Brown in attendance somewhere or other. All in all, Jimmy, there is no escaping your conclusion, and I'm prepared to accept it.'

'Yes,' replied Lavender, 'it's pretty certain; but the fellow must be made to betray himself. We haven't enough to go on, as it is. It's dangerously near being guesswork. You asked Crown about the baroness' papers?'

'I did. He has them in safekeeping. Not a thing in them, he says, that gives us a clue.'

Lavender smiled. 'There wouldn't be,' he rejoined laconically. 'Anyway, I've been through them twice, myself.'

'However, I told him of the fragment of paper Russell gave you,' continued Rittenhouse. 'It startled him.'

'When are you going to tell me?' I demanded, at this juncture. 'Where do I come in, Jimmy? Can I do nothing?'

Lavender turned to me very seriously.

'The fact is, Gilly,' he said, 'you will be a much better witness in all that is to follow, if you know nothing for a while. You can do one thing, though; you can keep an eye on me! I mean it. The fat is in the fire, if I'm not mistaken, and from now on, I shall be a marked man. I shall go calmly about my business, as if all were well, and it is up to you and Rit to see that I don't get a knife in my back, or something equally unpleasant. Rit and I know the murderer. The question is: does he know that we know? I don't think he suspects Rit; but he may suspect me. And the more innocent you appear, Gilly, the better it will be all around. But keep your eyes open.'

'All right, Jimmy,' I replied obediently. But I was horrified by the turn the case was taking, and for a long time I sat and thought deeply, while the two curious fellows who were with me actually sat and talked about baseball.

Who, by any chance, could have committed the crime? Who had the opportunity? I faced the problem squarely, and admitted that there were plenty of persons who could have done it. In addition to the great numbers of obscure passengers, first and second class, who had not even been named in the inquiry, there were undoubtedly half a dozen principals who might very well be definite suspects. The second class outfit, I was inclined to disregard, for a second class passenger surely would have been noticed by one of the stewards, if he trespassed on holy ground. And yet, as I came to think of it, was there so much difference between a first and a second class passenger? Actually, I was forced to admit, there was none, so far as appearance was concerned. Of the principal figures, however, five at least, as I now numbered them, stood forth clearly as possibilities. All had been, or could have been, near the scene of the murder at the time it occurred. And with something of a thrill, I realized that I must add young Russell to the list. I did not for a moment suspect him, but for that matter I hardly suspected any of the others.

And Lavender was in actual, active danger of one of them! Clearly, there was only one thing for me to do, and that was to watch everybody. I resolved to watch the entire ship from the captain down, not excluding Rittenhouse himself. Since I was to be Lavender's guardian, by Heaven, I would suspect everybody!

In this frame of mind, I went to bed and dreamed a mad, fantastic dream in which the captain of the liner, which curiously had become a pirate ship, stole into Lavender's stateroom and stabbed him with a fragment of paper, while the Baroness Borsolini joined hands with Rittenhouse and danced around them. Waking with a start, I sat up and listened. Finally, I knocked three times on the wall of my cabin, and listened again. After a pause, there came back to me Lavender's reply, in similar code. And after this performance, I turned over and managed to get to sleep.

The morning of the fourth day broke clear and fair and cold. I went at once to Lavender's room, to find him already up and gone. He did not appear until breakfast, and I had no opportunity to ask him where he had been; but it occurred to me that he was not playing fair. If I was to guard him against assassination, he ought at least to keep me posted as to his movements. So I thought.

Breakfast passed with the usual chatter about the uppermost subject in everybody's mind, and at a table not far removed from ours sat Murchison, the Iowa clergyman, eating his first meal in the saloon. He looked pale and thin, but happy to be on earth and able to eat. Later, I saw him in conversation with the purser, and still later with the captain. Was he, then, the heart of the mystery, and were the coils beginning to tighten?

Lavender too had a brief talk with the captain, after which they vanished in company, while Rittenhouse and the purser talked in low tones at the door of the latter's office. Obviously, something was afoot, and I felt strangely out in the cold. Then Mrs. Rittenhouse, and her sister, Miss Renshaw, corralled me, and for an hour I was forced to sing the praises of my friend Lavender to their admiring accompaniment.

After this, however, the suppressed excitement seemed to loosen up, and for an entire day the routine of ship life went quietly forward with only casual mention of the crime. Some gaiety was even apparent in the lounges and smoking-rooms, and I reflected sardonically on the adaptability and the callousness of human nature. The fifth day would be the last on board, for the sixth morning would bring us into port. It was this knowledge, I suppose, that cheered the passengers, although the Lord knew that the voyage had been anything but boring.

When I asked Lavender what progress had been made, he answered merely that he was 'waiting.'

★ ★ ★

On the fifth morning, I suddenly remembered that the day was the anniversary of my birth — not a particularly significant occasion, Heaven knows, but at least a subject for trivial conversation. Lavender, however, greeted the tidings with singular enthusiasm, and promptly ordered a splendid dinner for the evening; Rittenhouse ordered wine during the afternoon, to drink my health, and Mrs. Rittenhouse and her sister embarrassed me immensely by presenting me, with ridiculous speeches, with tiny bottles of perfume and post-shaving lotion, purchased of the ship's barber. The dinner went off with gusto, with everybody ordering champagne and making idiotic addresses, to which I lamely responded. My humble birthday, indeed, was made an occasion for strained nerves to relax and for worried men to forget their problems. To cap the climax, when I went to my cabin in the evening, there was a gorgeously wrapped and tied box of cigars and cigarettes, with the captain's card attached to it, and a huge box of candies, with the purser's compliments similarly presented. I felt excessively guilty about these latter gifts, feeling as I did that they were intended to show appreciation of Lavender's services. Lavender, however, only laughed and was pleased that my birthday should have passed off so well.

'Any occasion is good for a celebration, at sea,' he observed.

Late in the afternoon, we had dropped anchor in the outer harbor of Cherbourg, while a tender took off our passengers for Paris. Then, with a fresh breeze, we had headed for England and the end of the voyage. I had noted that, during the transfer of passengers for France, Lavender stood at the gangplank stretched between the steamers, and carefully observed every person who went aboard the tender. For a time, I had looked for fireworks, but apparently there was no call for his interference.

We sat late that night, upon the deck, the three of us, and for a time the purser made a quartette. It was with reluctance that Crown took his departure.

'We dock in the morning,' he said, as he prepared to go. 'I've a nasty report to make to the company, Mr. Lavender. You haven't anything to tell me that will make it easier?'

'The report will be full and complete,' replied my friend. 'The murderer will be apprehended at quarantine, by Scotland Yard officials, and the jewels will be turned over at that time.' Crown was startled and amazed.

'You don't mean to say that — that you've got your man!'

'Not yet,' said Lavender, 'but I shall certainly get him. Crown, he is one of the officers of this ship.'

The purser's jaw dropped; his fat cheeks sagged. His eyes searched the eyes of Lavender.

'My God!' he said. 'I'm almost afraid to ask you — who he is!'

Suddenly he got to his feet. 'Will you come to my cabin?' he asked. 'This is no place to discuss what you have to tell me.'

Lavender nodded his head and stood up. They moved off together in the direction of the forward deck.

'Ready, Gilruth!' said the Major, sharply, and I saw that his face was hard and set, his limbs braced. 'After them quickly.'

The sudden intelligence seared my brain like a hot iron, and then I went cold. But Rittenhouse was already on his way, and mechanically I followed him.

We were none too soon. Lavender and the purser had barely disappeared beyond the cheek of the wireless cabin, when the huge criminal fell upon his companion. There was a shout, and then a scuffling of feet and the sound of blows. The next instant, Rittenhouse and I were on the scene.

In the deep shadow of the piled lifeboats, a desperate struggle was in progress, with the rail and the water dangerously close. Even as we reached them, the wrestlers pitched toward the edge; the great bulk of the purser was forcing the slimmer figure of Lavender back over the rail. I heard the cold rush of the water, and the heaving breathing of the combatants. The wind snatched away my cap, and tingling spray beat upon my face.

Then Rittenhouse was upon the purser like a wolf, and with cleared wits I was beside him, aiding.

The powerful Crown fought like a maniac, but the odds were now against him, and slowly we wore him down. Haggard and disheveled, he struggled to the last. At length, Rittenhouse tripped him and brought him down with a thud that seemed to shake the deck. Kneeling on the great heaving chest of the beaten man, the Major forced the purser's wrists together, while Lavender snapped on bracelets of steel. As the struggle ended, Captain Rogers and his first officer ran up out of the shadows.

'Mr. Crown, Mr. Crown,' panted the captain, 'what is the meaning of this?'

But as the purser could only glare and foam, Lavender, slightly breathless, replied for him.

'It means, sir,' said he, 'that Mr. Crown has just been frustrated in an attempt to throw me overboard. Major Rittenhouse and Mr. Gilruth prevented him. As I explained to you, our actual evidence was slight, and it became necessary to force Mr. Crown to incriminate himself. The attempted murder of James E. Lavender will do for the present charge. Later it will be changed to something more serious.'

The first officer was incredulous.

'Do you mean,' he began, 'that Mr. Crown had anything to do with — ?'

'I believe the murder of the Baroness Borsolini to have been accidental,' answered Lavender. 'None the less, it was Mr. Crown who committed the crime.'

Suddenly the fat face of the prostrate man wrinkled like that of a child, and the great frame began to heave. Then sobs of anguish broke from the lips, and incredible tears rolled down the massive cheeks.

'I didn't mean to kill her,' sobbed the purser. 'I swear to God, Captain, it was an accident! I never meant to kill her. So help me God, it was an accident!'

5

With the purser safely locked in his room, under heavy guard, Lavender, in the captain's cabin, repeated the tale as chronologically it should be told.

'The Baroness Borsolini,' said he, 'was really Kitty Desmond, a well-known adventuress. Crown has made a full confession to me and to Rittenhouse. Miss Desmond was made the repository of the stolen Schuyler jewels, and sent to England with them, where they were to be sold, I imagine, and the money divided. She recognized me when I came on board, and wondered if I were on her trail. It worried her, and she made the bold play of coming to me with a cock-and-bull story of attempted theft, in order to find out what I knew and, if I knew nothing, to gain my sympathies. I am convinced that there was no attempt on her room, the first night.

'Crown, however, recognized her. She

had been a frequent voyager on the Atlantic, and many men knew her. She had been pointed out to Crown, a year ago, on another ship. He knew only that she was a police character, and probably up to no good. When I sent her to him, to test her story, she was obliged to carry the thing through, and tell him the same story she had told me. She trusted Crown's office, as she had every right to do, and actually deposited the jewels there, and received the usual receipt.

'But the temptation was too great for Crown. He was desperately hard up — deeply in debt — back home in England. It looked to him like a sure thing. He would keep the jewels himself, steal the receipt, which had been issued to Kitty Desmond, and defy her to say anything. He was, of course, in a position to fix the records in his own office, and being a matter of routine no one else likely to remember the issuing of that particular receipt. There could be no appeal for the woman; her story would be laughed at, if she reported it, for her reputation was against her. Probably she would accept the inevitable and make no outcry.

'Crown's slip occurred when, on the second night, he stole the receipt which had been given her. She woke up, and to keep her from screaming, he choked her. His reputation depended upon his silencing her, at least until he could talk to her. If he had not killed her, he would have offered her — when she caught him in the act of theft — a share of the profits. Unfortunately, she died under his hands; he is stronger than he suspects. He got the receipt, however, and fled. No one saw him; he had timed everything very well.

'As it happened, in giving young Russell a false address, the night before, the Baroness — so to call her — had torn off a fragment of the receipt, the only piece of paper that came to hand in the darkness. Whether she knew what it was, or not, we shall never know. Perhaps she did, for she tore off only a small piece; not enough to spoil the receipt. But there was enough of the print on the reverse of the written address, for me to guess what the entire paper must have been. If then, she had deposited something with the purser's office, the purser had lied when he told me she had not. In the circumstances, the logical conclusion was that she had deposited the jewels.

'Crown is a bold man, and he played his part well, once he was forced to it. But in the end, I let him know, through Rittenhouse, the importance I attached to a certain fragment of paper. As he had the rest of the paper himself, he knew very well what it was that I had, and what I probably suspected. He tried to bluff it through, even tonight, for he wasn't positive that I knew, and he had destroyed the rest of the receipt. Nevertheless, he was badly frightened, and he had already resolved to get rid of the jewels, and try to clear his skirts.

'As for me, my case was purely circumstantial, and would have been difficult to prove in law; I had to force Crown to incriminate himself. I told him pointblank, just before he sprang upon me, that he would be arrested, told him where the jewels were, and asked him what he intended to do about it. You know the rest.'

'And a wonderful beginning of your vacation it has been!' I said bitterly, looking at his lacerated hands.

'Don't be silly,' said Lavender. 'I never enjoyed myself more in my life. This has been just what I needed. And I'm sure the sea air, as a background, has been very beneficial to my nerves.'

'But where are the jewels?' asked the captain suddenly.

'I asked Gilruth to bring them with him,' replied Lavender with a smile. 'As a last resort, Crown tried to get rid of them, as I said, and so he palmed them off on Gilly. The birthday gave him his chance. The jewels are at the bottom of the box of candy, which was the purser's gift to my friend.'

Whereupon, I emptied the box onto the table; and the chorus of exclamations that followed were Lavender's reward for his efforts, and the final proof of the truth of his deductions, even though later the suicide of Albert Crown made legal proof unnecessary, and made unnecessary the prosecution of that unfortunate man.

We do hope that you have enjoyed reading this large print book.

Did you know that all of our titles are available for purchase?

We publish a wide range of high quality large print books including:
Romances, Mysteries, Classics
General Fiction
Non Fiction and Westerns

Special interest titles available in large print are:
The Little Oxford Dictionary
Music Book, Song Book
Hymn Book, Service Book

Also available from us courtesy of Oxford University Press:
Young Readers' Dictionary
(large print edition)
Young Readers' Thesaurus
(large print edition)

For further information or a free brochure, please contact us at:
Ulverscroft Large Print Books Ltd.,
The Green, Bradgate Road, Anstey,
Leicester, LE7 7FU, England.
Tel: (00 44) **0116 236 4325**
Fax: (00 44) **0116 234 0205**

ANGEL DOLL

Arlette Lees

It's the dark days of the Great Depression, and former Boston P.D. detective Jack Dunning is starting over after losing both his wife and his job to the bottle. Fresh off the Greyhound, he slips into The Blue Rose Dance Hall — and falls hard for a beautiful dime-a-dance girl, Angel Doll. But then Angel shoots gangster Axel Teague and blows town on the midnight train to Los Angeles . . .

THE INFERNAL DEVICE

Michael Kurland

Professor Moriarty, erstwhile Mathematics professor, is not 'the greatest rogue unhanged' that Sherlock Holmes would have one believe, but rather an amoral genius — and the only man Holmes has ever been bested by. *The Infernal Device* takes Professor Moriarty from London to Stamboul to Moscow and back, Sherlock Holmes close on his tail, until they both join forces to pursue and capture a man more devious and more dangerous than either of them has ever faced before . . .

I AM ISABELLA

V. J. Banis

It seems an innocent enough deception — pretend to be the absent heiress, Isabella Hale, just for one evening. And certainly the objective is a noble one — to present a generous check to an unquestionably deserving charity. As it turns out, however, Carol Andrews' identity is not the only thing that isn't all it seems. In no time at all, she finds herself in a high-stakes game of deceit and danger, in which she faces the ultimate penalty — death . . .

GUILTY AS CHARGED

Philip E. High

A self-confessed murderer recounts the events that led up to an apparently unprovoked attack; a gruesome murder scene holds nasty surprises for the investigating officers; a man makes what amounts to a deal with the devil — and pays the price; caught up in events beyond his control, a bit-part player in a wider drama has his guardian angel to thank for his survival . . . These, and other stories of the strange and unaccountable, make up this collection from author Philip E. High.